11/7   25p

Miss Aurelia Sinclair has just a year to repair her fortunes: unless she can find financial help, her father's Jamaican estates are forfeit to his creditors and Aurelia will lose everything. Risking all, she decides to set sail for London to find a wealthy backer, and to do so she poses as an heiress of unimpeachable background.

Unfortunately, fashionable London assumes that the rich Miss Sinclair is in search of a husband, and who more eligible than the dashing Harry, Viscount Belphege? Aurelia's mission comes close to failure when she realises that her time is running short—and that she has fallen in love with the man whose offer she has spurned already!

G000089858

Summer
Heiress
Ann Hulme

MILLS & BOON LIMITED
London · Sydney · Toronto

First published in Great Britain 1981
by Mills & Boon Limited, 15-16, Brook's Mews,
London W1A 1DR

© Ann Hulme 1981

Australian copyright 1981
Philippine copyright 1981

ISBN 0 263 73547 8

The text of this publication or any part thereof may not
be reproduced or transmitted in any form or by any
means, electronic or mechanical, including photo-
copying, recording, storage in an information re-
trieval system, or otherwise, without the written
permission of the publisher.

This book is sold subject to the condition that it shall
not, by way of trade or otherwise, be lent, resold,
hired out or otherwise circulated without the prior
consent of the publisher in any form of binding or
cover other than that in which it is published and
without a similar condition including this condition
being imposed on the subsequent purchaser.

Set in Times Roman

Photoset by Rowland Phototypesetting Ltd
Bury St Edmunds, Suffolk
Made and printed in Great Britain by
Cox & Wyman Ltd., Reading

CHAPTER
ONE

THE sun, streaming through the louvred window shutter, threw stripes of dark and light across the cluttered desk and on to the black silk waistcoat of the thin man who sat behind it. This man pulled a large cambric handkerchief from his pocket and mopped his brow fretfully. It was uncommon hot. From outside in the dusty, sun-drenched street the many and varied sounds of busy Kingston penetrated to this, his inner sanctum. Cart-wheels creaked and donkeys brayed. A babble of voices filled the air.

He did not feel well. He was afraid it was the begin-ning of the fever. He suffered from recurring bouts of a low fever which rendered him shivering and incoherent. He put away the handkerchief and said irritably, "My dear young lady, I cannot express it plainer! The time allowed for the repayment of the money has elapsed. Your late father . . ."

He broke off, uncomfortably aware that his visitor was staring at him in a very direct manner. He looked at her gloomily. She was a very pretty girl in pink muslin and a straw bonnet. Pretty girls, Mr. Ribble reflected glumly, had caused a great deal of trouble throughout the history of man, beginning with Eve, who, no doubt, had been just such a pretty young thing. He himself was a churchwarden, a respectable family man, a land agent of many years' repute and experience. Pretty girls, therefore, represented to Mr. Ribble every kind of human failing, from temptations of the flesh to a general confusing of judgement resulting in bad business decisions and altered wills. This young lady had a cluster of very attractive glossy black curls showing beneath the brim of the straw bonnet, and it was a very pretty bonnet, with taffeta ribbons.

Mr. Ribble made a great effort to frown and straighten his spine. "Miss Sinclair!" he intoned severely, sounding, even to his own ears, as though he was about to embark on the First Lesson. "There is nothing to be done. You must surrender all your properties here in Jamaica. It will do no good to argue with me."

"Indeed, sir?" said Miss Sinclair militantly. "I see no need to argue. You are incorrect in what you say."

Mr. Ribble almost choked. "Incorrect? *Incorrect?* Allow me to tell you, Miss Sinclair, that I have practised my profession here in Jamaica, and before that in England, for five and twenty years. If you fancy I am unaware of the exact situation, then permit me to disillusion you. Your late father offered all of his property as security for a very considerable loan, not one penny of which has been repaid. With the accumulated interest, the sum now owed . . ."

"You are incorrect, sir," persisted the young lady calmly, interrupting him with perfect *sangfroid*. "The time has *not* elapsed. Despite your refusal to grant me an extension, I still have until December 31st, 1818. It is but January."

Mr. Ribble permitted himself some small sarcasm. "I stand corrected, Miss Sinclair. You plan, then, to raise the money before the year is out?"

"I do," Miss Sinclair said purposefully.

Mr. Ribble almost forgot the symptoms of his fever in an unworthy feeling of malicious joy. "Here in Jamaica, my dear?" he purred. His yellow, parchment-skinned cheeks cracked into what, in another man, might have been a smile.

"No," said Miss Sinclair, rising to her feet and gathering up her reticule and parasol, "in London. I have booked my passage and sail with the tide." She swept out.

Mr. Ribble shuddered slightly as the door snapped shut. He stretched his hand down to open a door in the side of his desk, out of which he took a glass and the rum bottle. He set the glass before him and splashed a generous measure into it, spilling only a little on to the desk top. He was a temperate man, as befitted his activities as a churchwarden, but even he was convinced that the only medicine a European could rely on to combat the ailments which attacked him in the West Indies, was rum. In deference to his own reputation and convictions, however, Mr. Ribble dripped a small amount of water into his rum. He, at least, was not like those hard-drinking planters who drove, red-eyed beside their tight-lipped spouses, into Kingston in their polished carriages of a Sunday morning to attend divine service. He had responsibilities—and those responsibilities dictated that he should write to England on the subject of Miss Sinclair.

But the fever was gaining on him fast. He was in no condition to write a letter in time to catch this sailing. If Miss Sinclair wished to take herself off to Europe and be a sugar heiress for a summer, then let her. It would give him some peace. Nor would Miss Sinclair find it so easy to make her mark in English society as she obviously imagined. He, Ribble, was going home to bed. In an automatic gesture, he locked the rum bottle away and tucked the key into his waistcoat pocket. He might take a drop for medicinal purposes, but he intended to see that his clerks did not. He reached for his hat with a shaky hand and in an unsteady voice called for his pony and trap to be brought round. He dismissed Aurelia Sinclair from his mind.

The clock on the gilt-legged table ticked monotonously. Distantly, from behind the tightly-closed windows, the rattle of passing carriages in the London street outside permeated through to the morning room where the sunlight shone palely on the polished walnut and heavy damask. Lady Belphege lifted the reading-glass which lay on the table by the clock and held it over the letter in her hand.

"Aurelia Sinclair," she read aloud, squinting at the blurred script and holding both letter and magnifying glass out at arm's length. "Sinclair? I know no one by the name of Sinclair. What is this letter, Julia?"

"I do wish you would have spectacles made, Mama," said her one remaining unmarried daughter, in a depressed voice. "That reading-glass is useless." She glanced at the ticking clock. Already half-past eleven and the day's correspondence hardly touched. If only Mama would hurry a little. She would be late, and Antony would be waiting.

"I do not require spectacles," her mother said crushingly. "And do attend to the matter in hand, Julia. Who is she, this Aurelia Sinclair?" Lady Belphege laid down the letter and glass. "Well?" she demanded impatiently.

"Captain Sinclair's daughter," said Julia weakly.

"Don't show yourself so foolish as you are, ninny!" snapped her mother. "If I don't know who Miss Sinclair is, then how should I know who Captain Sinclair is?"

"Was," corrected her daughter. "The late Captain married Miss Hortense Falcombe, of Penzance."

"Hortense Falcombe!" exclaimed Lady Belphege, startled. "I haven't heard a word from or about Hortense for twenty years."

"Quite, Mama. It seems she married Captain Sinclair—it's a naval rank, apparently, not a military one—and went to Jamaica with him."

"What on earth for?" demanded Lady Belphege. "Typical. Just like Hortense. No sense. None of the Falcombes had any sense. They all made bad marriages and lived to rue 'em! So I suppose this gal, this Aurelia, is the product of that curious union, is she?"

"Yes, Mama. In her letter, if you read it . . ."

Lady Belphege tapped the paper by her hand irritably. "You've read it. I haven't the patience. What does she want?"

"To be introduced to polite society, Mama."

"By me, I take it?"

"Yes, Mama. She explains in the letter that both her parents now being dead, she has returned to England from Jamaica and, finding herself alone, has taken the liberty of addressing those of her mother's girlhood friends whose names she knows."

"Odd, very odd," said Lady Belphege thoughtfully.

"She really has no other course of action," said Julia, "if she has no family here at all."

"Does she state that she has no relatives of any kind?" asked Lady Belphege, and without waiting for an answer, continued, "Naturally she has to approach someone but it is odd that she should choose me. Why should she even know my name? I quite lost contact with Hortense long before her marriage. However did she come to give my name to her daughter?"

"I'm sure I don't know, Mama."

"I will see her!" pronounced Lady Belphege suddenly. "Write and tell her she may call. But I promise nothing. Make that clear. And now you may put all the rest of the correspondence away. You are driving me quite distracted with your fidgeting and watching of the clock. I will have my chocolate now. Tell Addams to bring it in straight away."

"Yes, of course." There was an unmistakable note of relief in Julia's voice. She acted as her mother's secretary, largely because Lady Belphege was too mean to pay for a service which could be had for nothing. Nor would any paid secretary have borne the brunt of Lady Belphege's ill-humour for so long. Julia gathered up all the different pieces of correspondence they had been discussing and hastily began to put them away.

"Where is Harry?" her mother asked suddenly, a peevish note entering her voice.

Caught off guard, Julia dropped a few sheets of paper and made a great play of picking them up. "I . . . I really can't say, Mama."

"I haven't seen him for nearly two weeks!" the old lady declared querulously. "Is he in Town?"

"I believe so, Mama."

"Gallivanting, no doubt. Too busy with his worthless friends and fancy women to come and see his own mother!"

"Harry does not fritter away his time in low society," declared Julia stoutly. "If he has not called, then I'm sure . . ."

"Oh, don't defend him! Write him a note—a stiff note. Say I demand that he calls on me within a week." Lady Belphege grasped the silver-headed ebony cane resting against her chair and tapped imperiously on the floor with it. Various indentations scarring the polished wood in the same area indicated that this was her usual practice.

"Very well, Mama," Julia agreed doubtfully, knowing that the very last way to bring her erring brother to see his mother was to order him to attend.

"I won't be ignored!" said Lady Belphege grimly. "Tell him so!"

"Don't I know it?" her daughter muttered rebelliously beneath her breath.

So Julia wrote to her brother, the Viscount Belphege, as directed, and she also wrote to Aurelia. Her letter to Harry was opened, read, and used to mark a place in a book. Her letter to Aurelia Sinclair had a very different reception.

"At last!" cried Aurelia aloud when the maid in the lodging house where she had taken rooms brought her Julia's letter.

"Been waiting for that letter, miss?" asked the maid. She gazed admiringly at the young lady, wishing that she too had those lustrous black curls and clear white skin. Funny, she mused, you'd think a fine young lady like that would be staying in a real nice house with rich people, not in rooms here.

"What?" Aurelia recollected where she was. "Oh, yes, yes. Thank you. You can go." She sat down and with trembling fingers broke the seal and opened out the letter. During the last months before her final illness her mother had talked a great deal about her early years in England. Aurelia had made a great effort to remember the names her mother had mentioned and since her own arrival in England she had spent the time diligently hunting up these ladies, now the mothers of grown families, and had written to them all. So far her letters had been ignored or answered with a curt refusal. Now, perhaps, at last . . .

"Oh, please don't let her refuse me!" Aurelia begged silently of Heaven. She read the letter hastily. "I may call! She will see me!" Aurelia jumped to her feet and made a little dance round the room, waving the letter triumphantly.

From the far corner came a rustle and the noise of a tongue clicked in disapproval. A stout, middle-aged woman, whose pink and white West Country complexion had not been entirely destroyed by the long years of exposure to sun and fevers, folded her hands tightly across her starched white apron and said: "That there letter be no good to you at all, Miss Aury. Just looking at 'un do give me a bad feeling."

"Oh, Sarah! Don't be so glum!" Aurelia came to a halt and waved the letter defiantly. "This is just what I need. You know why I've come to England. How am I to get the money if no one will introduce me to the places where it may be found?"

Sarah Fraddon shook her head of thick, iron-grey hair. "It don't seem right, miss. And one thing I do be sure of, neither your poor mam—sweet soul that she was—nor your pa, who had his faults but was always a true gennelman, would look kindly on what you've in mind to do. So there!" And Mrs Fraddon folded her arms and nodded her head to lend emphasis to her words.

"Papa would approve!" returned Aurelia undaunted. "Papa always said a person should be prepared to risk everything to save what he truly cared for."

"'Tisn't my place," said Sarah, growing animated, "to speak ill of your pa. But he 'risked all' well enough, and lost 'un. You be set fair to do the same, I tell 'ee. Why, when you was a little maid you was a harum-scarum little thing, and the years a'n't brought you no sense. I be responsible for you, girl! I be the only living soul left to keep an eye on you, and I reckon 'tis a punishment for my sins, I do. I left my home and my old mother to go with your mam to they West Indies in 1797. Many a time I thought I should have died, what with the turrible storms we did have on our way there, and folk goin' down like skittles wi' yellow fever all around once we did get there! But the good Lord has spared me to come home again, and I promised my poor dear lady, your mam, on her deathbed as I'd look after you. 'Tis my duty to tell 'ee, you'm fair set to land yourself in that much trouble, 'tisn't no way you'll ever get out of 'un.''

Slightly dampened but still optimistic, Aurelia sat down on the side of the bed and said brightly, "I'm not doing anything wrong, Sarah. You make it sound as if I was about to commit a crime."

"Young ladies don't sit on the bed!" Sarah observed snappishly, as if that itself was a crime. "There's chairs a-plenty."

Aurelia obediently removed herself to the nearest chair. "What I am doing," she said persuasively, "is done every day by men of business, and in the most respectable connections. I promise I will be careful."

"First you do talk to me of risking all, and now you'm on about being careful! If'n that don't just show that you don't know what you're about, my dear girl, then I don't know what does!"

"I'm going to call on her, anyway," said Aurelia stubbornly.

Three days later a well-dressed young woman in a blue gown with long, tightly fitting sleeves, a lace shawl and a fashionable bonnet with a pleated silk brim and a curled feather, trod daintily up the steps to Lady Belphege's front door and rang the bell. "Miss Sinclair," she told the butler with cool aplomb.

"Her ladyship is engaged at the moment, madam," she was told. "But if you would care to wait, I will tell her you are here."

He ushered her into a morning-room and left her while he went to convey the news of her arrival to his mistress. Aurelia looked around her, noting the signs of wealth and impeccable lineage. A pair of paintings depicting a lady and a gentleman in the fashions of the Restoration hung either side of the fireplace, and a set of Chinese vases and other valuable nick-nacks lay carelessly about. A French ormolu clock ticked on a nearby table and beside it lay a silver letter-knife and silver inkstand, both embossed with an unfamiliar crest, no doubt that of the Viscounts Belphege.

Aurelia felt a surge of panic. Perhaps, after all, Sarah was right and she should not have come. But she quelled these cowardly feelings instantly. After all, what had she to lose?

Suddenly, from behind the door to the hall, the sound of arguing voices burst upon her ear. It sounded as though at least two people were descending the stairs and coming towards the room where she was. Aurelia clutched her shawl nervously.

"Devil take it!" roared a man's voice. "Am I to be bullied?"

A woman's voice replied placatingly, "No, Harry dear, but Mama . . ."

"I have never failed in my duty to my mother yet! But for pity's sake, Julia, she'd have me call on her every blessed day!"

"You are the only boy, Harry. You know we girls don't count with her, and me least of all because I never caught a husband! It's you she wants to see."

"I'm sorry, Julia," the man's voice said more gently. "I know Mother treats you abominably. You don't have to put up with it, you know. You can come and live with me and keep my house."

"Thank you, Harry. But you'll marry one day, and your wife won't want a sister-in-law running her house!"

"I've no plans to marry, Julia. You can believe that."

"I do. But you are thirty, Harry, and you'll have to settle down some time. Besides, there is the question of an heir. Only you can provide that."

There was a long pause, as though Harry had a reply to that but did not feel he could express it before his sister. "My mother has other grandchildren to occupy her," his voice said at last. "Let her concern herself with Kate's children."

The footsteps approached rapidly, and Aurelia jumped back from the door, afraid that she might be caught eavesdropping. She was just in time. The door was flung open to reveal a small, plump, pale young woman with frizzy, mousy hair and a pleasant, worried face, rather like a small pug dog. Behind her stood a tall gentleman. Both stared at Aurelia.

"I'm so sorry," Aurelia faltered. "I was waiting . . ."

The pale young woman hurried forward. "Are you Miss Sinclair?"

"Yes. The butler . . ."

"My mother was occupied," Julia said hastily. "Please forgive us. My brother was just . . . May I present my brother, Lord Belphege, to you? I am Lady Belphege's daughter, Julia Trehowan. I wrote to you."

She moved aside and the tall gentleman strode into the room and bowed curtly to Aurelia. "How d'ye do, ma'am! I trust our noisy conversation didn't disturb you?" His voice was brusque and he stared at her very sternly from beneath thick black brows which gave his face a forbidding look. His displeasure at finding someone on the other side of the door was quite obvious.

Aurelia gulped and wished she could 'cut and run'. He was obviously a gentleman of fashion, elegantly attired in a well-cut blue coat, pale yellow breeches and gleaming top-boots. He was also strongly built and of commanding presence, and just now he was extremely angry. "Indeed, sir," Aurelia attempted to assure him, "I could hear nothing!"

He did not pretend to believe her, but gave her a very sharp look which made her wish not only that she had never come to this house, but that she had never left Kingston. "My sister had better take you along to see my mother, then!" he said coldly.

Aurelia allowed Julia to lead her away, uncomfortably aware that Lord Belphege's gimlet eye tracked her departure until she was out of sight.

"Creeping about with an ear to the keyhole, b'gad!" muttered Lord Belphege to himself when Aurelia had gone. "Heard every word we said, I'll swear. Now, what would a pretty girl with a curious nature want with the old lady?"

"So, Miss Sinclair, you want me to bring you into London society?"

Aurelia, sitting primly on the spindly chair opposite, could not help but stare, fascinated, at the elderly lady before her. Lady Belphege had been a great beauty in her far-off youth and traces of this could still be seen. She was still elegant, despite the rheumatism which, on 'bad' days, almost crippled her. She dressed with care, choosing to wear shades which flattered her. Her silver hair mounted in intricate coils which never moved, but there was a sharpness in the eyes under the strongly marked brows which reminded Aurelia forcibly of the lady's son. She pulled herself together and said, "I have made so bold as to write to you, madam, because you and my mama . . ."

"Ah yes, your mother!" Lady Belphege interrupted her. "It is many years since I had any news of Hortense. Have you been long an orphan, Miss Sinclair?"

"My father died two years ago, ma'am, in 1816, and my mother last year."

Lady Belphege said nothing, reserving her condolences, and Aurelia was forced to plunge on, not quite sure what she was expected to say. "My mother had always intended that I should come to London, into Society. So I . . . I left my estate and properties in the care of a capable agent and I came."

At the mention of the words "estate" and

"properties" Lady Belphege's eyebrows, which contrasted strikingly with the shining silver waves and coils of her hair, rose imperceptibly. "I hope your agent is a trustworthy man, Miss Sinclair?"

"Oh yes, utterly. My father retained him many years ago," declared Aurelia, closing her eyes mentally against the picture of the drunken incompetent who held this post in reality.

"Sugar?" enquired Lady Belphege.

"What? Oh yes, sugar cane."

"I see." Lady Belphege eyed the girl before her. One thing, at least, was not in doubt. This was Hortense Falcombe's daughter. The Falcombes had all lacked sense, but not looks. A Cornish family, they had all had the dark curling hair inherited by this child, the creamy complexion and fine violet eyes. Lady Belphege ran a practised eye over her visitor, noting the small hands and good teeth. Such details were important, many a girl's chances had been ruined because she had had big feet. This girl had no such obvious blemishes, and society was always willing to smile upon a pretty face, Lady Belphege knew that. Besides, if the child had inherited a tolerable fortune . . .

The planters of the West Indies were notoriously rich. Some of them lived like Eastern potentates, or so rumour had it. She made a quick calculation. Hortense must have been all of thirty-five years old when this girl was born. Were there other children? Delicately Lady Belphege asked, "Have you no brothers or sisters, my dear?"

"I was an only child, ma'am, I have nobody."

So the inheritance, whatever it had been, had not been divided. This child was sole heiress. Lady Belphege took matters a stage further. "Your mother's family, you have not been in contact with them?"

Her visitor flushed slightly. "My mother's marriage,

ma'am, was not to the taste of all of her relatives."

"Yes, I seem to remember," Lady Belphege said, frowning slightly as she attempted to dredge up isolated incidents of scandal from the past. Had not Hortense, to put it vulgarly, run off with some half-pay captain? Yes, of course. Well, it was the sort of idiotic, romantic thing Hortense would have done. No doubt she had been completely ostracised by her family after that.

"Besides," her visitor pursued as if to assure her that the scandal of her parents' misalliance was not the sole reason why she had not turned to relatives, "such connections as I might have on my mother's side are all in the West Country."

"And of little use to you there!" observed Lady Belphege in a matter-of-fact voice. That she could understand. This child had not made the long and uncomfortable voyage from Jamaica simply to shine in the limited society afforded by Exeter or Truro. "And your father's family? What were his origins?"

"My father never spoke of his family, ma'am," said Aurelia awkwardly, realising that lack of information here might weigh heavily against her. "I believe he was from Gloucestershire and entered the Navy very young as a midshipman, when he was only twelve years of age. After that he saw very little of his home."

'And no doubt,' thought Lady Belphege, supplementing this meagre detail by her knowledge of the World, 'he also married to vex his family and was probably cut off with a shilling. Still, he will not have been the first, nor the last, and it need not weigh against this child. She is frank, at any rate, and does not disguise the fact.'

"So, my dear," she said aloud, graciously. "I am extremely sorry to hear of poor Hortense's death. I should be glad to help her daughter in any way I can, but"—she held up a hand as Aurelia opened her mouth

to speak—"I do not enjoy the best of health these days."
Lady Belphege indicated the ebony stick leaning against
her chair. "And I am therefore limited in what I can
offer to do. I am afraid, my dear, that I am no longer able
to gad about quite as I did!" And here Lady Belphege
smiled for the first time.

Her visitor, in some confusion, hastened to assure her
that she would not have troubled Lady Belphege if she
had known of her disability and quite understood that
it would not be possible for the lady to undertake
strenuous social engagements simply to help a total
stranger. But the stranger would, all the same, be
eternally grateful for any introduction . . .

Lady Belphege cut short this flow. "I did not say I was
a recluse, my dear. I entertain at home and always hope
to see my house tolerably full, and I do attend functions
elsewhere whenever it is possible, so no doubt we shall
be able to do something for you. Now, on Thursday
evening next I am giving a very small affair involving a
few friends and acquaintances. Perhaps you would care
to come? Do you dance?"

"Yes, ma'am, moderately well," replied Aurelia,
reflecting that dancing indicated not such a small affair
after all, and that there would probably be upwards of
sixty to seventy guests at least.

"Waltz?"

"I can, ma'am, if it's allowed," Aurelia replied
cautiously, not sure whether this elderly lady still
objected to the waltz.

But Lady Belphege was not one to lag behind fashion,
whatever her personal opinion, and she said briskly,
"Good! Everyone waltzes nowadays and it is a great
disadvantage not to know the steps, though I confess I
am delighted that I am too old and indisposed to be
obliged to attempt the matter myself. I shall be pleased
to see you on Thursday, Miss Sinclair."

This was a signal that the interview was over and Aurelia left, highly satisfied. When she had gone Lady Belphege turned to her daughter, who had sat silent throughout the visit, and asked, "What do you think of the gal, Julia?"

"She seems pleasant and well-mannered," Julia said expressionlessly.

Lady Belphege was not to be misled by evasive answers. She pounced. "You don't like her, eh?"

"I . . . scarcely know, Mama. After all, we know nothing of her really. Do you think it wise to take her under your wing?"

"Oh, I have not done that!" returned the old lady blandly. "But I want to see more of the gal. She has intelligence and resource, and I like that. I cannot abide these witless, giggling, pert young misses who seem to abound on every side these days! I cannot but feel that the country is going to the dogs. It would not have been so in my young days."

Lady Belphege seized her cane and rapped it sharply on the floor, making yet another indentation on the parquet. "It all began with that sorry revolution in France! Not only the lower classes but people of quality too behave as it pleases them. However, Miss Sinclair, possibly because of her Jamaica upbringing, seems to have avoided the general addling of brains which has taken place in decent society here! Besides, she is very pretty, and everyone will like that. Though I doubt you do, miss!"

Julia flushed at this unkind thrust. "I have long accepted the fact that I am very plain, Mama. I do not envy others their good looks!"

"Then you would have the disposition of a saint, and I doubt that you have that!" snapped her parent. "Of course you envy Miss Sinclair, and all those like her! And so you should. Indeed, I never thought that *I* should have given birth to a child so plain!" She stared critically at her daughter.

"Well, Mama, it cannot be helped," her daughter returned placidly, regaining her composure. "Let us be thankful that all my sisters are handsome."

"Handsome is as handsome does," muttered Lady Belphege, not to be mollified. "They are all handsome and all fools, especially Kate. Only Harry has looks *and* brains, of all my children!"

"Yes, Mama," said Julia, who was quite prepared to agree with her mother on this point.

CHAPTER
TWO

LORD BELPHEGE, subject of his mother's approbation, was well known to be an obstinate, hard-headed and occasionally ruthless man; although his many friends were equally prepared to sing his praises too, as being generous to a fault when convinced the cause was genuine, and surprisingly considerate and kindly towards those in a weaker or less fortunate position than himself. His strong will had enabled him, at an early age, to hold his own against his forceful mother. His father had given up the unequal struggle quite early on, and Harry had inherited the title while still a youngster. Titled, rich, handsome and single, it was inevitable that he should be flattered, sought after and favoured. It was a wonder that he had not been completely spoiled. But Lady Belphege, realising the pitfalls into which her darling might so easily fall, had taught him in the nursery to distinguish between the genuine and the false, and the simple but hard fact that when strangers seek you out and wish only to oblige you, it is generally because they hope you will oblige them. "Mother trained me well," Harry was wont to observe. "I have developed an instinct about these things. I can always tell if something is not quite right!"

It may have been this instinct or it may have been Aurelia's pretty face, but Harry spent the next two days thinking quite a lot about his chance meeting with Miss Sinclair. He had learned, via Julia, that his mother had invited Aurelia to her house on Thursday—and today was Thursday. So Harry promptly made up his mind to attend the gathering himself. That would enable him both to please his mother and to take another look at Aurelia, who intrigued him. He scented a mystery. Pretty and assured young women, with just the right degree of modesty to prevent them being labelled 'forward', did not drop from the sky, nor even off the Jamaica packet.

He knew his mother was no fool, and so he was not unduly worried. But then, his mother was also getting along in years, perhaps a little less sharp than she had been once (although, to be sure, there was no sign of mental decay in Lady Belphege), and possibly a desire to help the daughter of a former girlhood friend might blur her judgement. Besides, Julia, whose judgement was not blurred in Harry's opinion, was uneasy about Miss Sinclair. Harry, therefore, meant to find out exactly what had brought the pretty heiress all the way from Jamaica to his mother's door. As a preliminary to his investigations he decided to pay a call on a friend.

"Harry!" exclaimed the stocky man in his thirties. He looked surprised but pleased. He had a friendly, plain face, rather red and weatherbeaten as if he spent much time out of doors, and was comfortably if a little untidily dressed in clothes which, for all their deceptive simplicity, came from the hand of a very good tailor.

Harry shook Antony Helliwell's hand heartily and apologised for bothering him. "I heard you were in Town, Tony. What's brought you? I thought you'd be settled comfortably on a river-bank to fish or be out shooting harmless pigeons."

Helliwell looked a little confused and said, "I don't spend all my time doing that. Sit down, Harry. Don't stand on ceremony! What can I do for you?" He looked expectant, rather like a well-trained gundog, as if he hoped the game would be flushed and he would be able to do just what his visitor wanted.

"Tony," the other said easily, "I'm after information, and I've come to seek your aid."

"Information?" Antony waved his hands deprecatingly. "If it's about horses, Harry, I'm your man. I flatter myself I know horseflesh. But if it's about anything else, I'm about as useless a person as you could hope to consult. What is it? Buying a racehorse? Looking out for a matched carriage pair?"

"Nothing like that, I'm afraid. Tony, your family owns land in Jamaica, isn't that so?"

"Well, yes," Antony looked startled. "My father owns a couple of sugar cane estates. He has a few other interests too. I don't know much about Jamaica, though. Although I was born there, you know, but the climate proved unsuitable for my mother, and so, when I was just a babe in arms, she brought me back to England to live and I've never been back to the West Indies. The best I can do is to quote you the price of raw sugar on the London market. Father knows all about the place, though, because he continued to live out there alone for a number of years and didn't return permanently to England until he was ready to retire from his colonial occupations. Why the interest? You're not thinking of packing up and moving to the colonies, are you?"

"Well, not yet, anyway," grinned his visitor. "Not until London gets too hot to hold me! You mention sugar cane—a number of fortunes rest on sugar, I believe. All the West Indian planters are as rich as Nabobs, they tell me. Is it true? Would you say the word 'sugar' implied a sound financial background for a person?"

"It should," Antony said. "Do you want facts and figures? I can get them for you."

"No, thank you, all the same. It's not the sort of

information I can get from bankers and dealers that I'm seeking. What I really want to know is whether you, or your father—how is he, by the way?—would know the name Sinclair."

"Sinclair or St. Clair?" asked Helliwell practically. "One word or two?"

"I really don't know," said Lord Belphege, momentarily taken aback. "One word, I fancy. S-I-N-C-L-A-I-R."

Mr. Helliwell thought and slowly shook his head. "No, I can't say I do. Something to do with Jamaica, is it? Because I can ask the old man. He's pretty well, by the by, apart from a gouty foot. He doesn't get about much, but usually knows what's going on."

"The Sinclair I'm referring to," Harry said, and then paused to walk to the barometer on the wall and stand before it, apparently studying it intently. His listener waited. "Was," Harry continued, apparently to the barometer, "a Captain Sinclair, now deceased, who is said to have owned land and property in Jamaica, including at least one sugar cane estate. He had a wife called Hortense, also now deceased, and one daughter, who is now in London."

"If the Sinclairs own land in Jamaica then my revered parent will know of them. All these planters' families know one another, and our agent, Ribble, who manages our interests out there, keeps Father informed as to all the local gossip. Father was altogether twenty years out there, and still wants to know all the births, deaths and marriages. Is that the sort of information you want?"

"That's exactly what I want!" Harry turned his back to the barometer and smiled warmly at Mr. Helliwell. "And I'd like to know something about the Sinclair properties."

"It may take a little time to find out," Antony warned him.

"Never mind, so long as I get what I want," said Lord Belphege with the calm assurance of a person who generally does.

His friend looked at him a little curiously. "Business matter?"

He did not think so for one moment. His was an uncomplicated mind, but even he knew that Harry was not likely to be obsessed by the current price of sugar cane. Gentlemen of fashion did not involve themselves with the discreet enquiries, the mean haggling, of the financial world. They had their men of law and their harassed agents to do these menial, if essential, tasks for them. They, quite rightly, concerned themselves with their tailors, their stables and their mistresses.

On all these things could a gentleman concentrate without embarrassment. But Lord Belphege had not instructed his man of affairs to contact the Helliwell man of affairs . . . he had come hot-footing it round to Mr. Helliwell's comfortable rooms in person. It was, therefore, a very personal matter which had brought him. Mr. Helliwell was both human and curious.

Lord Belphege was indeed looking faintly taken aback at the notion that he might suddenly have decided to dabble in trade. "Oh, no, no," he said, shaking his head. "A trifling matter . . . for my own satisfaction."

Now Mr. Helliwell looked embarrassed. "Sorry. Didn't mean to pry! Oh, Harry . . ." His expression of acute embarrassment increased.

"Yes?"

"Er . . . how is your mother?"

"Fit as a fiddle and just as hard on the ear!" Harry said carelessly. "Rheumatics, of course."

"Oh, is she?" said Mr. Helliwell a trifle gloomily, adding hastily, "Oh, good! I'm glad she's well . . . rheumatics aside. And . . . um . . . your sister?"

"Which one? I've got seven."

"Lord, so you have," the other agreed, with a touch of commiseration in his voice. He himself was an only child. "I've only ever, er, had the honour to meet Miss Julia Trehowan."

"Julia's the best of 'em," Harry told him, "and she's under Mother's thumb."

"I know," said Mr. Helliwell darkly. "She's well, though?"

"Who? Julia? Certainly. Fit as a . . ." he paused, recollecting he had already used the simile 'fiddle', and so finished, rather ungallantly, ". . . fit as a flea!"

"Excellent!" said Mr. Helliwell doubtfully, as if he was glad to hear the lady in good health, but not sure whether he would have compared her to a small insect himself.

"Well, I'll be off," said Harry, picking up his hat and cane. "Have some dinner with me next week, Tony? A piece of roast beef, a bottle or two of good wine?"

"Glad to. I'll write to my father about your Sinclair family."

"Thank you, Tony. I'm much obliged to you." Lord Belphege put on his flat-topped demi-bâteau, adjusted its curling brim to a rakish angle, tucked his cane under his arm and departed, whistling. Strains of *I'm bound for the Rio Grande* floated up the staircase.

"See here, my lovely," wheedled Sarah Fraddon, "you don't want to be going to a place what'll be full o' strangers. 'Tidn't right. 'Tidn't seemly."

"To be sure, Sarah, I'm never going to get there at this rate." On her knees in front of her open travelling trunk, Aurelia, in her petticoats, rummaged furiously in its depths. "Oh, Sarah! We can't *possibly* have left my cerise dancing slippers behind in Kingston!"

Sarah heaved a disapproving sigh and went to produce the slippers from the bottom of a cupboard. "'Tidn't no use, Miss Aury. See here, this 'un is worn into a hole, right on the toe."

Aurelia seized the slipper and gazed at it wildly in near despair. "Oh, Sarah! What shall I do?"

"You could stay at home here," suggested Sarah.

"Sarah, I am going. Will you darn this slipper, please?"

Sarah hesitated. "I don't know that I will, Miss Aury. The whole business don't seem right to me."

"Then give it back to me and I'll do it myself!"

But this was poaching on Mrs. Fraddon's preserves. "That you will not, missie. That's my job, and though I do say it myself, tidn't no one can do a neater bit o' darning than Sarah Fraddon."

She sat down with needle and thread and darned the slipper almost invisibly while Aurelia struggled unaided into a cream silk evening gown with a low-cut square neckline, puffed sleeves and flounced hem.

"Hook me up, Sarah please!"

Sarah looked up from her work and let out a shriek. "Bless us, my dearie! You'm not going like that?"

"Of course I am. Why ever not?"

"Why not? Because tidn't decent, that's why not. See here, my girl, you're to put a bit o' lace or something over the bosom. I'll swear, the gennelmen will be able to see . . . well, I won't say *what*! Here, let me . . ."

"Let it alone, Sarah! It's perfectly respectable and all the ladies will have gowns cut as low as this. I don't want to appear a dowd."

"Ladies, is it?" observed Sarah. "Tidn't no way for a lady to dress, to my mind. And neither your mam nor your pa would want to see you showing yourself in public dressed like that! You do look proper fast."

"I do not!"

It took much further wrangling before the dress was finally hooked up and a cerise sash carefully tied round the high waist. Aurelia's hair was secured with no fewer than thirty pins, and the girl came up from below to say that the hired cab was at the door.

Sarah, watching the cab roll away across the cobbles, shook her head. "Just like her pa! Those Sinclairs, they just head for trouble natural!"

"Ah, Harry!" said his mother graciously as he bent to kiss her thin white hand. "How *nice* to see you at one of my little evenings! Such a rare pleasure." She was seated near the doorway, her cane at her side, her upright figure giving no hint of the crippling affliction which plagued her.

He smiled at her disarmingly. "Now, now, Mama! When have I ever failed you?"

"Constantly!" she said dramatically. "But I shall forgive you. Not that you deserve to be forgiven. Only stand by me for a little while and help me greet my guests."

"Can't Julia . . . ?" He glanced over his shoulder.

"Harry!"

"Oh, very well, madam," he said resignedly. "For five minutes."

"My dear boy, I would not detain you for longer," she said serenely. "Five minutes will be quite sufficient."

"By *my* watch, madam!"

Mother and son glared at each other in an affectionate clash of old and devoted foes.

"Naturally, Harry my dear!" said Lady Belphege sweetly, conceding the first round.

Lord Belphege shook a few male hands and kissed a few female ones and made an assortment of banal remarks to a selection of dull faces and then consulted his fob watch.

"Don't be so obvious about it, Harry. It makes such a

bad impression. Surely five minutes with me isn't so tiresome?" his mother enquired archly.

"I assure you, madam, that was not my reason for looking at my watch. I was just wondering . . ."

Another guest arrived, and what Harry was wondering was left unspoken.

"Ah!" Lady Belphege said suddenly, tapping his arm. He bent his head to where she sat, still rigidly erect, on the gilt chair. Perhaps only he guessed the effort of will that upright posture demanded from her. "Here's something curious!" she whispered in his ear, pointing with her fan towards the door. "D'ye see that gal in cream with the cerise sash, just come in?"

He followed the direction of the fan and his expression brightened. "Ah, yes, Miss Sinclair!"

"How do you know?" demanded his mother, annoyed at having her air of mystery broken.

"I have already met Miss Sinclair briefly."

"Where, pray?"

"Here, Mama, in your very own morning-room."

"Then you do not need me to present you, sir!" said his mother tartly.

"No, Mama, I fancy I may present myself. Will you excuse me?"

Aurelia glanced about her nervously. She knew nobody here and nobody seemed disposed to pay her any attention. She knew she must go and pay her respects to her hostess, but Lady Belphege was whispering to her son. Both were looking towards her and, oh horror, here came Lord Belphege himself, making a beeline straight for her. If she had known he would be here then she might well have heeded Sarah's advice to stay at home.

"Good evening, Miss Sinclair," he said affably. Considering that the last time they had met he had looked very angry, this time he looked positively friendly.

Aurelia was not deceived. Despite the smile of welcome he was beaming down on her, she would as soon have offered her hand to a 'tame' leopard. She forced herself to hold out her fingers gingerly. "Good evening, sir," she said suspiciously.

"I was hoping *you* would be here!" he said cheerfully. The contrast with his previous brusque manner was startling to the point of mystery. He took hold of the tips of her fingers and raised them briefly and gallantly to his lips.

Taken aback, Aurelia said, "Me, sir?" in a lame voice.

"Oh, yes."

"Why?" Miss Sinclair asked bluntly, retrieving her fingers, which he was still holding, and putting her hand behind her as though afraid it might be bitten off at any moment.

He burst into laughter. "You receive compliments very crushingly!"

"Not at all. I didn't realise it was a compliment!" she defended herself.

"Ouch!" he said, wincing. "I'm losing my touch. Am I such a social oaf?"

Aurelia blushed crimson, her cheeks clashing nicely with her cerise sash. "I didn't say that. You misunderstand me."

"But I do not *want* to misunderstand you, Miss Sinclair," he assured her earnestly, repossessing himself of her hand. "Do come and say all the right things to my mother."

Convinced that she was being mocked and bright pink with humiliation, Aurelia allowed herself to be led to Lady Belphege.

"How nice to see you, my dear," said Lady Belphege. "Harry, you may let go of Miss Sinclair's hand now. I'm sure she isn't going to run away."

In fact, Miss Sinclair looked very much as though she would like to run away.

"You look very charming, my dear," said Lady Belphege appraisingly. "I am not generally fond of false curls on young girls, but I admit they do suit you."

Aurelia started and blurted, "Beg pardon, ma'am, but they aren't false, they're my own!"

From behind her she heard Lord Belphege chuckle.

Lady Belphege delicately raised an eyebrow. "Then you are to be complimented on an abundance of very pretty hair."

Aurelia was reduced to the silence of miserable confusion, believing that Lady Belphege must think she had courted this compliment deliberately.

"Introduce Miss Sinclair to some young people, Harry," commanded his mother. "She knows *nobody*."

With this final thrust metaphorically protruding from between her shoulder-blades like an arrow, Aurelia was led away on Lord Belphege's arm. Lady Belphege sighed. "How tiresome!"

Julia, who was standing nearby talking to Antony Helliwell, hastened across to her mother, wondering what was wrong now. Really, Mother was always finding fault. "What is tiresome, Mama?"

"To be a victim of one's own vanity, child! Here am I, fondly imagining that Harry came tonight to please me, and in fact he came to see Miss Sinclair."

Julia's normally pale face flushed. "I doubt it, Mama."

"Ninny!" said her mother. "Have you no eyes in your head? Nor brain either?"

Julia wriggled. It was so embarrassing when Mother criticised her before others. If only she would lower her voice . . .

"To whom are you talking?" demanded Lady Belphege. "Antony Helliwell, isn't it?"

"Yes, madam."

"I can't abide that man. He smells of the stables. Who invited him?"

"I. . . I thought . . ."

"You did, did you? Still looking for a husband at your age?"

"Mama, I am only thirty-two!"

"When I was thirty-two," said her mother waspishly, "I had eight healthy children and had buried two sickly ones."

"I know, Mama. I am one of those children and I do remember all the others!" retaliated her daugher, in the nearest she had ever come to open revolt.

Lady Belphege stared coldly at the rebel. "Do you, miss? Well, don't imagine that I'm going to allow you to marry Antony Helliwell! I won't have that red-faced yokel in the family."

"Mama, he isn't a yokel. The Helliwells are very respectable and own considerable property in . . ."

"Don't argue with me!" snapped Lady Belphege. "Go and fetch me a glass of wine."

"You know, Miss Sinclair," Harry said, "I have always been fascinated by the notion of going and living in a sunny climate, like Jamaica, for instance."

"Have you?" replied Aurelia disbelievingly.

"And I long to hear all about it from you. Let us sit down. I'll fetch you an ice."

"No, thank you."

"Don't you care for ices?"

"Yes—I mean, no! It's too much trouble."

"Oh, no trouble." He strolled across the room towards the table on the far side. Aurelia, whom he had left marooned on a sofa, stared about her wildly. She should have listened to Sarah. This was proving a perfectly dreadful evening. Why on earth couldn't that man go and harass someone else with his unwanted courtesies? And here he came again with the ice.

"Flavoured with rum," said Harry, setting a silver dish before her with a flourish. "A memory of Jamaica for you."

"Lord Belphege," Aurelia said with barely controlled anger, "I fancy you are hinting at something!"

He looked pained. "Not at all. I want to know all about Jamaica. Were you born there?"

"Yes, I was."

"And never been to England till now?"

"Never."

"You must find it very strange," he said, adding kindly, "Your ice will melt."

"I do!" said Miss Sinclair, attacking the ice viciously. "And some of the people here I find very odd!"

Harry grinned. "Now *you* are hinting!"

"If the cap fits. . .!" snapped Aurelia.

"The weather, now," he continued, unperturbed. "So chilly and damp here."

"Yes, it's horrible," said Aurelia.

"So . . . the climate is horrible and the people are odd. You must long to be back in Jamaica."

Aurelia put down her spoon and said seriously, "You know, that's absolutely true. Sometimes I wish I had never left."

He was silent for a moment and then asked unexpectedly, "Do you dance?" His voice sounded different, the mocking note had vanished.

"Not much," said Aurelia quickly, unwilling to be led into circling the floor in the arms of this amiable and smiling predator. The orchestra had struck up one of the new waltzes and several couples were swirling happily around the centre of the room.

"Don't they dance in Jamaica?"

"Yes, they do! Must you always be referring to Jamaica? We're not backward in the colonies, you know. Some of us can even read and write," she finished with heavy sarcasm.

"Aurelia," he said, "You don't mind if I call you Aurelia, do you? Just when we're alone, of course. Aurelia, I do hope we shall meet often!"

Aurelia glared at him, speechless.

"And now," he continued, "since you have finished your ice, I shall do as my mother bade me and introduce you to some people. Now, here is Gussie Foote." He hailed a very tall and languid young gentleman, resplendent in military uniform. "Miss Sinclair, may I present Captain George Augustus Foote? Gussie, this is Miss Sinclair, lately arrived from Jamaica. I know you will look after her." Smiling, Harry departed and left Aurelia to George Augustus.

"Sit down, may I?" asked Captain Foote in a bored voice.

"If you like," said Aurelia. "You are not obliged to, just because Lord Belphege requested it of you. I do not require company to be forced upon me."

"Nothing to do with that," he replied unperturbed. "My feet hurt."

"Oh!" said Aurelia, startled. "Then please do sit down at once!" She moved along the sofa to accommodate him.

He draped himself gracefully over the sofa, but even sitting down he still contrived to look very tall. He turned his head suddenly and caught Aurelia's critical gaze. "Something wrong, ma'am?"

"Oh no, I was just thinking that you are very tall."

"Six three . . ." said Captain Foote sadly. "Damned disagreeable."

"How so? Surely not."

"Look a fool on a horse. Stirrups dangle down either side. Makes a cavalry charger look like a nursery rocking horse."

Aurelia giggled. She was beginning to like George Augustus.

"Friend of Julia's, are you?" enquired her companion agreeably.

"No, I only know her very slightly," Aurelia said cautiously.

"Thought you couldn't be. Too pretty, for one thing, and too bright, for another. All of Julia's friends dashed dull. Keep telling her so. I tell her, get rid of 'em all and get a new set."

"People are not dinner plates!" cried Aurelia. "You don't turn out your old friends just because other people don't like them, and buy a new set!"

"Don't you now?" he said, a wicked glint in his eye. "Then, my dear, I'm afraid you will never get on in the World!"

"If 'getting on' requires me to discard all my friends to please people who don't give a fig for me, then I would be happy not to get on!" said Aurelia firmly.

"Stick by your friends, eh?"

"Yes," said Aurelia, adding a little sadly, "Only I don't have any in London."

"Better off without," he advised her. "Rum set of folk in London nowadays. Take a look around this room."

Aurelia looked at the well-dressed ladies and handsome gentlemen before her and sighed. The cream dress she was wearing was pretty, but not new, and she had trouble hiding the darned slipper. The air was filled with lively chatter, the sound of laughter, the tinkle of glass and the strains of music from the small orchestra, half-hidden behind an archway.

"Do you know who rules here?" asked Captain Foote pleasantly.

"I suppose Lady Belphege," she ventured in reply.

"By no means," he returned immediately. An impish smile tugged at the corners of his mouth. "This is part of the kingdom of old King Scandal! He rules here. What are they doing, all these elegant folk, eh? They are gossiping, Miss Sinclair. Telling tales out of school. Planning intrigues and conducting them, too, under the noses of us all. Whose husband with whose wife? Is Mr. X really Lady Y's new lover? Is it true that Lord Z has established his mistress in the family home?"

"They all look perfectly proper to me," Aurelia observed doubtfully.

"Ah, they look it, madam, but they ain't it! That is the secret of success in society today. There, I hand it to you on a plate, as it were. Discretion, ma'am, discretion! Discretion is the only virtue recognised here, and lack of it is the only vice! Conduct your affairs as you will, but do it with discretion!"

"You are very hard on everyone!" Aurelia reproved him. "Surely they cannot all be so immoral and loose-living?"

"D'ye see that pretty young thing in rose-pink over there?" he asked, nodding across the room.

Aurelia said she did.

"Sweet, ain't she?" he said. "She's a sort of cousin of mine. Just nineteen and as fresh as a daisy. Married last year. Can you pick out her husband?"

Aurelia hesitated, then, seeing the young lady in question throw a glance of unmistakable interest over her fan towards a handsome youth some yards away, she replied, "There, that gentleman in the blue coat, holding a glass."

He crowed in delight. "By no means, Miss Sinclair. The dandy in the blue coat is married to that plain girl in lilac silk. My cousin's husband is that odd old fellow over there, wearing, if you please, that outdated bagwig with three buckles of a side."

"But he is sixty if he is a day!" cried Aurelia.

"Sixty-three, ma'am, and as rich as Croesus. Both his

sons by his first marriage are older than their step-mama . . . and indeed, the youth in the blue coat is one of them!"

"Oh!" gasped Aurelia, turning scarlet. She fell silent and sat staring at the crowd before her. She became aware that Captain Foote was studying her closely, but when she turned towards him he dropped his thoughtful air and instantly resumed his foppish one.

"I don't believe you are really as bored as you look!" Aurelia told him.

"Can't help my face," he said apologetically. "If you ain't a friend of Julia's, then are you a protégée of the old lady's?"

"You mean Lady Belphege, I suppose. Not a protégée, no. But she and my mama were friends, years ago."

"Hum!" he said, stroking his chin. "Beg pardon for asking, my dear, but you aren't setting your cap at Harry, by any chance?"

"Certainly not!" spluttered Aurelia, so genuinely angered by such a suggestion that he hastened to apologise profusely.

"Terribly sorry and all that, but, y'see, when the old lady takes it into her head to put a girl forward, it's generally that she's trying to get Harry a wife and is trotting out another one for him to view."

"I'm not a horse," Aurelia said stiffly. "I'm not on view, and I wouldn't marry Lord Belphege if he were the last man on earth!"

"Tiresome!" said Lady Belphege again to nobody in particular.

"Oh, not again!" muttered Julia, a few feet away.

"Look, Julia," said Antony Helliwell nervously, "I'm sure your mother doesn't like my being here."

"Oh, pay no attention, Antony. It's just her disposition."

"Bit of a battleaxe, isn't she?" he whispered.

"Well, she . . ." Julia waved her hand ineffectually. "Harry can always manage her, he always could. She dotes on Harry. He shouts back at her."

"Brave fellow!" he said with feeling. He gave Julia a shrewd look. "Harry means a lot to you too, doesn't he?"

She looked surprised. "Yes, he does. I've never really got on well with any of my sisters. Their characters are so different to mine. We're all friends, you understand, but not *close*. I've only really ever been able to talk things over with Harry. Harry understands so well."

"He was getting some funny looks from that girl in the cream dress with the pinkish sash he was spending so much time with just now. Seemed to me there was a distinct lack of understanding there."

"Oh, that's Miss Sinclair," Julia said in an offhand voice. "She wrote to Mama and asked her to bring her into Society. She comes from Jamaica and her parents are dead."

He looked interested. "So *that* is . . ."

"Julia!" called Lady Belphege imperiously.

"I have to go," whispered Julia.

"Look, Julia, I'll slip away now, but I'll meet you tomorrow in the usual place, in the Park."

"I'll be there!" she promised.

"Why were you muttering with *that man*?" grumbled her mother.

"You mean Mr. Helliwell, Mama?"

"Ninny!" said her mother absently.

Julia flushed. "I do wish, Mama, that in front of other people . . ."

Her mother ignored her. "Men are so unpredictable!" she said fiercely. "I have been trying to find Harry a wife for the past eight years.''

"I know, Mama, and so does he."

"And now," continued Lady Belphege crossly, "I do declare he means to marry that child!"

Julia's jaw dropped. "Which child, Mama?"

"Aurelia Sinclair, ninny!" snapped Lady Belphege.

CHAPTER
THREE

EVEN supposing Lady Belphege to be right in her predic-
tion, Aurelia, at least, was blissfully unaware of any
complications of a romantic nature threatening the plan
she had hatched on the way from Jamaica to England.
Stage one of the plan had been achieved—she had been
introduced into polite society. Stage two involved comb-
ing that society for a suitably wealthy, but not over-
intelligent, person of either sex who might be persuaded
to lend a sympathetic ear to Aurelia's problems; and
Aurelia's problems, or rather Problem, pressed hard.
First, however, she had to establish herself in the social
round.

Lady Belphege continued to be very kind and sent
several invitations, and one or two other people began to
invite Aurelia too. It was not long before it became clear
that accepting all these invitations was going to be a very
expensive process. Aurelia had a fine skin and clear
complexion and so was spared the necessity for much
paint and powder. Sarah was skilled at putting up her
mistress's hair so that a professional hairdresser was not
required. But for a lady to appear twice at a ball in the
same dress would be unthinkable. Dainty slippers burst
at the seams after two wearings. Hairpins and rouge,
flowers false and real, shawls, gloves, reticules,
bracelets, fob watches and earrings. . . . The list seemed
endless and the cost enormous. Moreover, Aurelia had

no wish to run up bills in London which she would have had great difficulty in settling.

Nor, indeed, could she have done so. Titled ladies and the daughters of wealthy parents might run up huge bills. Pretty, youthful strangers with no family or friends to step in and settle debts were regarded with suspicion from the first. The slightest delay in settling an outstanding account would have meant that dressmakers, milliners, glovemakers and others would have declined, gently but firmly, to set another order in hand for her. So Aurelia and Sarah spent hours sewing on braid and unpicking flounces in an attempt to trim old bonnets and dresses to look like new, but that could not be done indefinitely, and Aurelia had noticed Lady Belphege's sharp eye resting a little curiously on one or two of her outfits.

She also found herself at a disadvantage in not having the same background and connections as other young ladies with whom she found herself mixing. They spoke of people she did not know. They discussed plays and operas she had not seen. They compared notes on their travels in countries she had never visited. One elderly lady enquired whether she had been to 'the Bath', and Aurelia, not realising this referred to the celebrated spa, almost made a dreadful *faux pas*, supposing her to be talking of a local bathing establishment. Some of these people, sometimes, asked polite questions about Jamaica, but it was easy to see their interest was feigned. They scarcely heeded her answers and soon began to speak of Venice and Florence or the beauty of the Alps or the invigorating air of Switzerland, none of which Aurelia had experienced.

She had begun to feel something of a country cousin and was therefore very pleased when she received a note from Lord Belphege in which he explained that he was escorting his sister Julia to the opera, and asked whether

Aurelia might not like to come too. Aurelia had just returned from a not altogether happy visit to Lady Belphege's house, where she had found two other ladies, of imposing fashion and devastating poise, who had been politely surprised to hear that Aurelia had never seen snow, and icily disapproving when Miss Sinclair said that she felt English children were so bundled up, poor things, that their limbs scarcely saw the light of day, and how nice it would be if the weather here were warm enough to allow children to run around barefoot in their petticoats.

So Harry's suggestion was very welcome. At least if she could discuss the opera there would be no raised eyebrows. Her eagerness to acquire the experience of going to the opera completely overrode any shyness or caution at the thought of being taken there by Henry, Viscount Belphege.

It was not to be expected that Sarah Fraddon would show the same enthusiasm for the proposed visit. "The theatre is a turrible place, miss! I mind the old rector, Mr. Wilkins, when I was a girl, telling us about 'un. 'Tis a haunt of sin, he said."

"How did he know?" countered Aurelia. "If he thought it so bad, I dare say he didn't go. And if he didn't go, how did he know?"

"'Twasn't necessary," said Mrs. Fraddon. "He'd seen the actresses what the fine gennelmen brought down to Bath for a bit o' sport. Fast hussies, every one. Painted, too. 'Jezebels' he called 'un."

"Well, I'm sure opera singers are quite respectable," Aurelia said firmly. "And I shall only see them, not meet them, and everyone goes to the theatre."

"Well, then, since you'm set on going," said Sarah stiffly, "what shall I lay out for you to wear?"

"My new dress," said Aurelia promptly.

There was a pause and they both looked towards the

chair in the corner of the room, over the back of which
lay a pretty gown in gold organdie, its satin sash hanging
over the arm of the chair and trailing on the floor. Sarah
clicked her tongue and bustled over to pick up the sash
and fold it tidily.

"I must, Sarah," Aurelia said in rather a subdued
voice. "I can't appear before Lord Belphege looking a
dowd."

"And if you'm invited to one o' they fancy balls or
high-faluting receptions?"

"Then . . . then we'll have to make one of the other
dresses over."

"My dear Miss Aury, you know as well as I do that it
can't be done, child."

Aurelia went to pick up the organdie dress and held it
up against herself. "It's the only one I haven't worn
before, Sarah. Julia has seen all my dresses, and don't
tell me she won't recognise any one of them if I put it on
again."

"You a'n't paid for that dress, Miss Aury," said Sarah
sternly. "Not yet, anyhow."

Aurelia was silent. "I will pay for it directly," she said
eventually.

"That's not my meaning, my lovely! O' course you'll
pay for it . . . you a'n't dishonest! But when you've paid
for it, what then?"

Aurelia laid down the dress carefully and pulled her
cotton wrap more firmly around her. She was in that
state known as 'undress' and preparing, with Sarah's
help, to face the day. She went to sit before the mirror
and stared at her reflection thoughtfully. After a moment
she put up her hand and pulled at the ribbon securing her
abundant black hair. It tumbled around her shoulders in
twisting curls.

"Sarah," Aurelia said slowly "how much would a
hairdresser pay for my hair?"

"Miss Aury!" gasped the horrified Sarah. "If you'm planning what I think then you'll do it over my dead body!"

"Short hair is still in fashion!" Aurelia said quickly. "I've seen several ladies with a head of short curls, or cut ragged, you know."

"Oh, my lovely," moaned Sarah, near to tears, "I've washed and brushed and plaited and dressed that pretty hair of yours since you was a baby . . . and now you sit there, calm as you please, and tell me you'm going to cut it all off and *sell* it!"

"Yes," Aurelia agreed calmly, "I am. With a little luck, people will notice my new 'head' and not my old dresses. Now then, here's how we'll do it. You go out and find a hairdresser and tell him to come up, or send someone competent up, immediately. When he's cut off my hair, collect it up carefully and follow him out on to the stairs and offer to sell it to him. It won't do, you see, if *I* try to sell it to him. Try to find a hairdresser who is also a wigmaker . . . then he's sure to be interested."

"Supposing he a'n't?" muttered Sarah unhappily.

"No matter. I shall have my new 'head' in any case, and that is my real purpose."

"There, mademoiselle!" said the hairdresser, stepping back. "It is finished!" He was an elderly Frenchman with a thin, birdlike face and deft movements. He held a hand mirror to the back of her head so that she could see the effect from behind.

"Thank you," Aurelia said soberly and Sarah let out a sob of despair as she bent to pick up the shorn tresses from the floor.

"You do not like it, mademoiselle?" the hairdresser enquired anxiously.

"Yes. You've done it very nicely, I'm sure," said Aurelia. "It does stick out a little oddly."

"Because it must be washed and dressed, mademoiselle. If you will permit me, and if your maid will bring us a basin of warm water and a little soap . . ."

Water was brought and the cropped head of hair washed and then twisted into curls and pinned into place.

"I shall return," said the hairdresser grandly, as he gathered up his scissors and combs, "and dress it for you when it is dry, mademoiselle. In two or three hours."

"Thank you," said Aurelia, still very sober.

He cleared his throat delicately. "Permit me, mademoiselle, to say you have a classic head. Such bone, such feature, such colouring . . . In my youth, dear young lady, I dressed the heads of the ladies in waiting to the Queen of France. I know what I am saying."

Aurelia looked at him with some interest. "Then you've seen many changes, monsieur," she said sympathetically.

He shrugged "What can one say? Some of those pretty heads I dressed tumbled on the guillotine. One lady sent for me from prison to build her a head so that she could mount the scaffold looking her best. I made her such a pretty head, with powder and flowers. I am sorry ladies do not powder their hair any longer. And as for the gentlemen . . . pah!" he looked disgusted.

"Then you do not care for the short hair such as you've cut mine!"

"Ah, for you, mademoiselle, it is different, because you have such good bone and you are so very young and full of life. The effect will be charming. I will come back in two hours and prove it so! Ah . . . the cut hair, mademoiselle . . ."

"Yes?" Aurelia asked calmly.

"You would not consider, mademoiselle . . . parting with it? There are many ladies, you understand, less fortunate than you, who require curls which are not their own.''

"Discuss it with my maid!" said Aurelia, with dignity and satisfaction.

When he had left she stared into the mirror in despair. Her head looked extraordinary, and she could not imagine it ever looking 'charming.' Even when Sarah returned triumphant, having driven a hard bargain for the shorn hair, she was not encouraged. But she was wrong. At the appointed time the elderly Frenchman returned, removed the pins and set to work with a comb and brush. To her astonishment and delight a cloud of glossy black curls rose beneath his comb like billowing waves. Even Sarah, who had been standing behind him to observe how it was done, relaxed her grim expression and replaced it with one of cautious approval.

"There!" said the hairdresser with satisfaction. "You like it, mademoiselle?"

Aurelia turned her head slowly from side to side. "I look different."

"But you like it?" he repeated anxiously, bending forward a little.

"Yes . . . yes, I think I do. Only I must get used to it."

"It will have to be trimmed at least every six weeks!" he warned her. "And if the curls grow limp, your maid can pin them up at night and your nightcap will hold them in place till morning. Your hair has natural curl, mademoiselle, you are fortunate."

Secure in the knowledge that her new 'head' quite altered her appearance, Aurelia ventured forth that evening in a gown she had worn twice before. It was one of her favourites in pale violet organza sprigged with tiny embroidered flowers and a velvet sash. Around her shoulders she had draped a long, narrow shawl of Spanish lace which she had brought with her from Jamaica.

Harry stared at her very hard. "You look very charming, Miss Sinclair!" he said at last.

Beside him, Julia fidgeted with her shawl and said, "Yes, you do," in a voice remarkable for its lack of enthusiasm. She was dressed very unbecomingly in a peculiarly unattractive shade of green, usually associated with sea-sickness, and her plump arms were bedecked with expensive and ugly bracelets. The gown's square-cut neckline was filled in with a bib of pleated muslin rising to a frill round Julia's short neck, which made her head look as though it rested directly on her sturdy shoulders without any intervening piece of anatomy at all. Her mousy hair was parted in the centre and dragged up into a topknot which had been augmented by a bunch of false curls. Atop the lot sat a spray of artificial cherries which succeeded in producing the general effect of a disarranged bird's nest, from which the occupant had fled in the middle of his dinner.

Not surprisingly, Julia looked awkward and unhappy. Aurelia wondered briefly why someone, her brother for instance, did not advise her. That bilious green, those clumsy bracelets on her chubby wrists, were glaring mistakes which could have been avoided so easily. Aurelia turned her gaze away in some embarrassment and found that Harry was still studying her. His eyes were on her cropped head. Aurelia flushed slightly and clutched her fan nervously.

"You have been persuaded to cut your hair," he said slowly.

"I . . . no one persuaded me. It was my idea," Aurelia stammered, a little unsure. Suppose he did not like it? Lord Belphege was very much a gentleman of fashion. If he did not like it, very likely others would not.

"It is very pretty," he decided at last.

"Do you like it really?" Aurelia asked him earnestly. "It seems very strange to me, I only had it done today.

Please be honest."

"I am always honest. I would not flatter you. If I did not like it, I would say so," he returned calmly. "I think it suits you very well. You will turn every head. No one will look at the stage or the poor singers!" He smiled briefly, his white teeth flashing.

Julia cleared her throat and said crossly, "May we not find our box, Harry? There you may sit and stare at Miss Sinclair's curls at your leisure! It is most disagreeable to be standing here, jostled by all sorts of people."

He raised his eyebrows slightly and said, "Of course, Julia. Come, Aurelia!"

Hearing her brother address their guest by her Christian name, Julia shot Aurelia a glance of deepest suspicion, but Harry had taken her arm was guiding her toward the staircase leading to the boxes. "I think Miss Sinclair is a little nervous, my dear!" he whispered into his sister's ear. "Be kind to her."

Julia almost growled. "To be sure, she does not look it!" she snapped in a muttered snarl. "Every man here has his eyes fixed upon her. I'm sure she cannot fail to be pleased with the effect she is producing!"

"Now, now, Julia!" he murmured, his voice slightly amused. "This is not you! You almost sound like Kate!"

Julia's mouth twitched in annoyance, but she made no reply.

There was ample evidence that Harry himself, at any rate, meant to be kind to Miss Sinclair. He insisted that she have the best seat in the box. He explained the story of the opera beforehand, lent her his opera-glasses and pointed out the most celebrated singers. He handed her her shawl and picked up her gloves and her programme when she dropped them. During the first interval he procured them cooling drinks. Aurelia was beginning to wonder how she had ever found him alarming and to enjoy the evening immensely. True, there was a minor flaw in the general atmosphere of harmony. Julia, though polite and careful to engage Miss Sinclair in conversation, was at the same time cool and distant in her manner. At first Aurelia put this down to a natural reserve, or perhaps misgivings over the bilious green gown, but after catching Julia looking at her in no very friendly manner for the second time, Aurelia began to wonder whether she had inadvertently committed some blunder which had offended Harry's sister.

She searched her memory but could not imagine what it could be. As a gesture of good intent, she offered Julia her seat.

"I'm sure you cannot see from there, Miss Trehowan. Do take this seat for a little. It really is not fair that I should have it all the time."

"Thank you, I can see very well! Please remain where you are, Miss Sinclair. It is your first visit to the opera, after all."

"Oh, but I shall come again, no doubt!" cried Aurelia, not with the best tact in the world. "We can change places as soon as the scene changes."

"Really, *no*, Miss Sinclair!" returned Julia quite sharply. "Do sit down!"

Aurelia sat down, rebuffed.

"Julia can have my seat," said Lord Belphege amiably. "Here you are, Julia, come and sit here." He stood up and handed his sister to his vacant chair before she could protest and then sat himself in her chair, just behind Aurelia's shoulder. "There!" he said cheerfully. He leaned forward and his breath touched lightly on the nape of Aurelia's neck. "Won't you take a look through the glasses again, Miss Sinclair?" Then, when Aurelia had taken them in her hand and was holding them to her eyes, he reached over her shoulder and added, "Allow me to adjust them for you." He bent his face close to hers.

Aurelia thanked him in some embarrassment and

Julia scowled openly. "Oh dear," thought Aurelia, putting up the opera-glasses to hide her face and her confusion, "she really does dislike me. Whatever for?"

Fortunately the second interval brought an unexpected diversion, though one not fully appreciated by Aurelia at the time. "Harry!" Julia urgently whispered. "It's William!"

There was some commotion going on in a neighbouring box, occasioned, it seemed, by the late arrival of two people. One was a very striking but rather sharp-looking young woman in a clinging gown of silvery grey silk with a very revealing décolleté. The other was a pale-faced man approaching middle age, whose general expression suggested he was about to be sacrificed in some particularly nasty manner by an especially unlikeable tribe of ferocious natives.

Julia gave a snort. "Only look at him, Harry. I declare, one doesn't know whether to laugh or cry! How can he cut such a figure in public?"

The pale man was handing his fair companion to her seat and she was making great play with her fan, holding it to her face and surveying the auditorium with her sharp eyes over the top of it.

"Has he seen us, do you think?" whispered Julia to her brother.

"Not yet, but his light-o'-love certainly has," he returned casually. "As soon as she has decided how to play the situation, she will inform him of our presence, no doubt." Lord Belphege yawned elegantly, a process which involved his putting his long fingers before his mouth. From behind his hand he whispered to Aurelia, "Pray don't think us unmannerly, Miss Sinclair! We have just observed a brother-in-law!"

"Is that gentleman married to one of your sisters?" enquired Aurelia, surprised. She tried to observe the pale man without staring at him and encountered instead the appraising eye of the damsel with the fan.

"He is, alas, poor fellow," said Lord Belphege uncharitably.

"But surely that is not one of . . ." Aurelia broke off in some confusion and coloured as she realised her *faux pas*.

"Quite right, Miss Sinclair!" he said with a touch of amusement in his voice. "That is not one of my sisters! That is his *chère amie*."

"Oh," said Aurelia, wondering what one did to be correct when brought face to face in company with a relative's mistress.

"Does he have to flaunt her so in public?" grumbled Julia. "He makes fools of us all!"

"By no means!" her brother disagreed equably. "He makes a fool of himself. Half of London has closed its doors to him already."

The female with the fan whispered into her escort's ear, and the pale man gave a start and shot a furtive look towards the box where Lord Belphege and his party were seated. Harry bowed politely towards him.

"Good evening, William!"

The pale man was seen to mouth "'Evening, Harry!", and then to fall back in his chair and look even more disconsolate than ever.

"Poor Billy, she'll do for him yet!" observed his brother-in-law *sotto voce*. "Are you thinking of taking a husband, Miss Sinclair?"

"What?" exclaimed Aurelia. "No, I'm not. No such thing, I assure you."

"Ah!" he said, amused. "You are a rare young lady. I thought that the Chase Matrimonial was the object of every young lady's thoughts."

"I cannot think why you should imagine that!" said Aurelia, rather cross at what seemed to her to be a slur on her own sex.

"Probably because a large number of young ladies pursue Harry himself!" Julia said silkily. She gave Aurelia a very hard look.

"Oh, I see," Aurelia nodded. "Yes, I dare say they do. You must be what they call 'eligible', Lord Belphege. I'm sure you're much sought after."

He passed a hand across his brow. "What I like about conversation with you, Aurelia," he said, "is that I get exactly the sort of answers I deserve."

There was a slight disturbance to the rear of them and a tall, lanky, familiar figure entered their box, bending his head awkwardly beneath the low, narrow arch. Aurelia had noticed his blue hussar jacket earlier and was not surprised to see him.

"Hallo, Gussie, what are you doing here?" asked Harry with pleasure. "I didn't know you had an ear for music. I would have invited you to join us."

"Lord, no, I haven't!" said Captain Foote feelingly. "Tone deaf. Can't make head or tail of it. How can a fellow who is dying run about the stage for ten minutes, singing his lungs out? I'm here doing my duty, escorting an elderly aunt. Hopes of her will, you know. I say, Harry, ain't that your whatsit, I forget his name, in the next box?"

"My brother-in-law. Yes, it is. He is trying not to notice us and we are being suitably gracious to him. Take good heed of him, Gussie, and mend your ways!"

"My ways," said Captain Foote with dignity, "are impeccably virtuous!" He turned to Aurelia and added in a stage conspirator's whisper, "What do you make of it, Miss Sinclair?"

"I'm sure it's nothing to do with me!" said Aurelia promptly.

"I meant the opera!" he explained.

Aurelia turned scarlet and stammered, "Oh, I see, I . . . I thought . . . Oh, yes, I like the opera very much. I think it's very fine."

"Do you, b'gad?" he said with interest. "I'd be glad if you'd explain it to me some day. Have you taken a look at that woman who keeps coming on and screeching?"

"Soprano, Gussie," said Lord Belphege patiently.

"The build of the woman!" Captain Foote observed in awe-struck tones.

"Now, Gussie, not before ladies!" warned his friend.

"I only asked if you'd looked at her!" said the Captain, aggrieved. "Lord, they're going to start up again. Duty calls! I must get back to my aunt. She's got an ear trumpet, you know. When she's tired of listening, she puts it down and can't hear a thing. Useful little gadget. Julia! Miss Sinclair!" He rolled an eye at Aurelia. "Often think of our conversation, Miss Sinclair!"

Aurelia flushed and opened her mouth, but he had gone. Julia gave her a further suspicious glare. Just at that moment Aurelia suddenly began to wonder whether the likeable Captain Foote might not have the answer to her Dilemma. When she arrived home that night she sat down and penned him a note, asking him to call.

CHAPTER
FOUR

AURELIA prepared her little sitting-room carefully in readiness for the arrival of George Augustus in it. She could have wished it was not so small nor so obviously dingy. However, Sarah had mended the curtains and cushions and brought in a vase of fresh flowers, and the housemaid had been persuaded, with a small largesse, to sweep it out especially thoroughly so that, all in all, thought Aurelia, it did not look so very bad. Anyhow, it told the truth and Aurelia was beginning to wish that she had done the same to Lady Belphege. Well, she hadn't lied, exactly. On the other hand, she had not explained her exact circumstances very fully.

"But I could not do otherwise!" she told herself for the hundredth time. To admit that every brick and every square yard of earth she owned were about to be forfeited to meet unpaid debts, would hardly have persuaded Lady Belphege to present Aurelia in society. Nevertheless, Aurelia was beginning to foresee certain complications in what had seemed, in Jamaica, an excellent plan. Not least amongst these was the awkwardness of explaining the wonderful plan to others, as she was about to do to Captain Foote.

Voices and footsteps could be heard on the stairs. "He's coming up!" exclaimed Aurelia, pushing Sarah towards the door. "Go and let him in!" She sat down on the little sofa and arranged her skirts elegantly. She was wearing a dark blue day dress with a white muslin fichu and sleeves *à la mamelouk*, puffed from shoulder to wrist by ribbons gathered at intervals the length of the arm. Aurelia was satisfied that she looked elegant, respectable and demure.

"Come right in, sir, won't you?" she heard Sarah inviting her visitor.

The Captain's tall figure in its ornate blue and silver jacket, white breeches and tasselled black hessians, wandered diffidently through the door. There was something so very unmartial in his aspect, despite his splendid uniform, that Aurelia had to make a great effort not to laugh. She gave him a welcoming smile and bade him sit down.

"You have not been inconvenienced, sir, by my asking you to call?" she asked anxiously.

"Well, ma'am," said the Captain, lowering himself cautiously into the unsteady embrace of the chair opposite to his hostess, "I was most flattered to receive your letter, of course, and dashed curious too, to be frank. I came straight away, as you see."

"And I do thank you, Captain Foote," said Aurelia earnestly. "The chair is quite safe. I examined it carefully before you came and it's quite solid. All the furniture here is rather old, as you see."

He glanced around but made no comment.

"Perhaps you would like some tea?" enquired Aurelia brightly. "I'm sure some could be procured."

"Thank you, ma'am, no!" he replied hurriedly. "I don't drink it."

"Forgive me," Aurelia said. "You are a soldier, I should have thought of that."

"Well," he said wryly, "I was in the Peninsula and in the Low Countries and believe me, we drank very little tea!"

"Were you in Spain, then?" Aurelia asked. "Was it very bad? They say it was."

"Bad enough," he said. "But I took a pair of grey-hounds along with me and managed to get in a bit of coursing."

"Oh!" said Aurelia, startled. "Well, that was nice . . ." This seemed to be the wrong remark to make of a battle campaign, so she asked him quickly whether he had also been at Waterloo.

"Yes," said the Captain thoughtfully. "Rum affair, that."

Aurelia shuddered. "Such a dreadful battle!"

"Um," said her visitor, adding sadly, "Sam fell early in the day, shot through the heart. I've never found another like him."

"A friend?" asked Aurelia sympathetically.

"Yes and no," he said. "My horse. Best cavalry charger I ever knew. Down he went, dead as a stone, and pitched me off into the mud. Left me wandering about for twenty minutes with bullets and muck flying all round me and then, a bit of luck, a riderless horse just trotted up beside me and stood there, lathered up to the ears and blowing. So I hopped up into the saddle. Then up trots a trooper. 'Is that you, Captain Foote?' says he, peering through the smoke. 'Well, it ain't Napoleon Bonaparte!' I said, and then I looked down at my uniform. Had to laugh. I was so covered in mud, I could have been anyone."

"I think," she told him, "that you, and all your comrades, were very brave and gallant men!"

Her visitor sank down in his chair and pulled at his moustache in a distressed sort of way on receiving this compliment.

Aurelia decided that the time had come to take the plunge. "Captain Foote, I'm sure you're wondering why I wrote to you."

"Yes," he said.

"You see," she told him seriously, "I feel that although you adopt the pretence of being flippant, you are to be trusted."

"Good Lord!" he exclaimed, starting back in his chair, which rocked alarmingly.

"I mean," Aurelia hurried on, "that I want to speak to you in confidence, and I couldn't do that if I thought you'd blab it all over Town."

Captain Foote gripped the arms of the chair and gasped, "Confidences, Miss Sinclair? Me? I ain't on for a lady's confidences!"

"No, no, Captain! You misunderstand. This is a business matter!" said Aurelia sternly.

"Ah," he said, relaxing his grip. He fixed a shrewd eye on her. "What's it all about, then, m'dear?" He stretched out his long legs and contemplated the gleaming toes of his hessian boots.

Aurelia clasped her hands together a little nervously. "You must understand, Captain Foote, that this is a very private matter. You may have heard that I own some properties in Jamaica."

"So I understand," he said, still staring at his boots.

"But what you don't understand," Aurelia said sadly, "is that I only own them in name. Some years ago my father borrowed a great deal of money, using the properties as security. He was given several years to pay it back and at the time, I suppose, he thought he could do so easily. But he couldn't and he didn't."

"And now, I suppose," interrupted George Augustus, raising his gaze from his boots to fix her with a very sharp blue eye, "the shark who lent him this sum wants his money back or your property."

"Yes, exactly. And I am quite determined that he shan't get my property!" Aurelia declared militantly.

"And how, forgive me, do you propose to stop him? If you haven't the money, that is?"

"That's what I want to explain. You see, there are

some houses in Kingston and a large sugar estate elsewhere on the island. The estate isn't paying very well. It
has been badly mismanaged and it needs money put into
it. But it *could* pay! Now, if someone would pay off the
loan, and then the estate were reorganised, perhaps one
or two of the Kingston houses sold, well, in a few years
he would have his money back with interest . . ."

" . . . and you would have your estate? My dear girl,
it's not on!"

"Why not?" demanded Aurelia. "It's a good estate.
And it's mine! No one is going to take it from me."

"Look, Miss Sinclair," he said, leaning forward in his
chair towards her, "suppose, now, that along comes a
fellow name of 'X' who agrees to advance you the cash to
pay off what you owe. Well then, now you owe that
money to 'X'. You're in the same position as before!"

"But I'm not!" argued Aurelia. "Because I will have
made a business contract with 'X' to develop my estate
and properties. He will be my business partner and we
will both make money."

He sat back in his chair and heaved a sigh. "You
weren't thinking that perhaps I might be 'X', were you,
Miss Sinclair?"

"It's really a very sound proposition," Aurelia
persuaded.

"It's a lunatic proposition! Beg pardon, my dear, but
if you go round London prattling like this, you will get
yourself locked up. You haven't told anyone else about
this, have you?"

"No, not yet," she admitted.

"Then please be advised by me, Miss Sinclair, and
don't!" he entreated her.

"Then what am I to do, sir? Let my estate go? I shan't!
You're a soldier! You were in the Peninsula and at
Waterloo. You know how to fight. So do I."

He scratched his chin and sat regarding her thoughtfully for a moment. "Some people would call you an adventuress, my dear," he said at last.

"I am not!"

"It's not what you are, m'dear, it's what you *seem* to be that matters!" he answered promptly. "This is London. This is the world of *Bon Ton*. Fashion. Society. They will call you an adventuress, if not worse."

"Will they?" Aurelia said, a note of doubt sounding in her voice. Her manner lost something of its former confidence.

He leaned forward again and said kindly, "See here, m'dear . . . I couldn't help you anyway. Second son, you know. I've got expectations, as it were, but no ready cash. Why do you think they put me in the Army? It's the golden rule—first son is the heir, second son goes into the Army, third son goes into the Church, you know. To make things worse, there is talk of disbanding the Eighteenth, so my prospects are hardly good for the immediate future. Of course, if all my relatives should catch some kind of plague and be wiped, every man Jack of 'em, off the face of the earth all at once, then it might be different. As it is, I soon might not even have a regiment."

"I thought, if you didn't want to do it yourself, you might know someone who would," Aurelia remarked in a small voice. "Someone who is a little of a gambler, perhaps."

"Or a little of a simpleton. No, no. If you will allow me to advise you," he spoke slowly, "what you really need is . . ."

"Don't tell me I need a good lawyer, for I'm sick of lawyers!" said Aurelia tartly. "They do nothing but discourage one."

"Not a good lawyer, my dear, a rich husband!" he said.

"But I don't want to *marry* somebody to get the

money!" cried Aurelia in exasperation. "That would be like selling myself. It would be horrible. And then you could call me an adventuress! I want a business partner!"

"Good grief, Miss Sinclair, a pretty girl doesn't have business partners! Or, if she does, she finds herself pretty quickly in the wrong kind of business. Now, listen to me, do. *I'd* marry you like a shot, only for the reasons already stated I won't fit the bill. Pity, but there it is."

"Thank you, anyway, for your kind offer," Aurelia said glumly.

"I regret deeply that it's not possible, I assure you," he said with surprising emphasis. "Because you're a remarkably fine girl, a splendid girl! But I haven't a penny and you haven't a penny, so it wouldn't do for a moment. No, Miss Sinclair, you will have to make a set at Harry."

"Make a set at Harry?" squeaked Aurelia in a rage-stifled voice. "Oh, really, Captain, I'm surprised at you!"

"At me?" he exclaimed. "By Jove, you do have a nerve, ma'am!" he paused. "Yes, you do have nerve," he continued, "and you deserve to be successful. I hope you are. I won't tell anyone of this business of your property. I just hope you won't tell anyone either, I mean, about this weird idea of a business contract. Naturally I am your servant, Miss Sinclair, and you may always call on me—not that I could necessarily help. And don't spit fireworks at me if I mention Harry again. Harry's taken with you, anyone can see it a mile off. And you can't say you don't know Harry is a pretty fine catch!"

"Let others angle for him, then!" said Aurelia stiffly. "I don't want to marry him. Nor do I believe for one instant that he is 'taken' with me. For some inexplicable reason, Lord Belphege finds me very amusing. I know he is laughing at me, even when he isn't."

"I don't follow that last bit," admitted her visitor, "but I do assure you that you're wrong." He stood up. "And now I must be off." He stared down at her from his great height. "Harry isn't a fool, Aurelia," he said seriously. "Perhaps you'd better tell him that you've no fortune and your properties are about to be the subject of a settlement for debt. Don't ask him to be your business partner, though! But it's always best to be quite on the level with Harry. He's not a fellow who likes to be deceived."

He left Aurelia to her thoughts: her thoughts left her very uneasy indeed.

It was the following Sunday that Aurelia, after leaving Matins, persuaded Sarah that it was such a pleasant morning that they might take a turn in nearby Hyde Park. Aurelia's description of the opera had done nothing to improve Mrs. Fraddon's opinion of that entertainment, and Aurelia had been forced to listen to much more of the late Mr. Wilkins' opinion on the theatre. However, at the moment there was an unspoken agreement between them not to refer to the vexed topic at all.

They strolled along sedately, Sarah marvelling at the sight of so many people "with nothing to do", and Aurelia busy observing the fashions. After a few minutes she saw two figures ahead of her, one of which looked familiar. It was a woman, and as she turned her head to look up at her male companion Aurelia caught her breath. Why that was Lord Belphege's sister, Julia!

Aurelia quickened her pace slightly and manoeuvred herself into a position where she could see Julia's escort. She did not know the man, but his face was familiar. He, too, had been at Lady Belphege's party, but had left early.

"Ha!" murmured Aurelia, scenting a hidden love affair. "I wonder if Lady Belphege knows her daughter is walking here with whoever-he-is?"

"Miss Aury, my dear!" hissed Sarah from the rear. "Walk proper! Dodgin' about like that, 'tis enough to make folks think you'm touched in the head!"

Aurelia slowed down and fell back beside Sarah. She did not want Julia to see her, which might be embarrassing for them all. After a while Julia and her companion, still in animated conversation, turned off down a side path and were lost to view amongst all the other Sunday morning strollers. Scarcely five minutes after this, the sound of hooves thudded close behind them and they were overtaken by a sole rider on a black horse. The rider reined in, took off his hat and bowed over the pommel to Aurelia.

"Good morning, Miss Sinclair!"

Aurelia stared up at Lord Belphege in some surprise. "Good morning, sir!"

He swung down from the saddle with easy grace to stand beside her on the footpath. "I'm very pleased to see you this morning, Aurelia, I was going to write you a note."

Sarah dug Aurelia painfully in the ribs and asked in a hoarse and perfectly audible whisper, "Who's this gennelman, Miss Aury? And what's he doing calling you *Aurelia*?"

Aurelia flushed. "Be quiet, Sarah! This is Lord Belphege."

"Well, you tell his lordship he don't have no right to call you *Aurelia*! If'n you won't tell 'un to call you Miss Sinclair, like 'tis proper, then I will!"

Scarlet with mortification, Aurelia turned to a highly amused Harry and said apologetically, "I'm sorry. This is Sarah Fraddon, who has been with my family since before I was born."

Harry was well used to the eccentricities of old family retainers, so he smiled now and said "I rather gathered that! Well, Aurelia—ah, Miss Sinclair!—I wanted to invite you to my eldest sister's house. Catherine keeps dull company but an excellent table, and who knows? It might amuse you."

"Thank you," Aurelia said doubtfully. "But does your sister want to meet me?"

"Oh, very much. I have been telling her all about you!"

Aurelia looked even more doubtful.

"Tuesday?" he asked. "I'll tell Kate and she will have her secretary send you a card."

"I . . . yes, thank you."

"Then I'll call for you."

"Maybe you will and maybe you won't!" said Sarah grimly. "And maybe I won't allow my young lady to accept your invitation!"

"Sarah. . .!" pleaded Aurelia in an anguished whisper.

"Don't you go and 'Sarah' me, my dear. You don't know what's proper. This smart gennelman, I take it, is the one as took you to the oper-y, that tidn't no fit place for any young girl. Now he wants to take you to his sister. Well, I want to know, what sister? Where does she live and is she a respectable and God-fearing woman?"

Aurelia wished the ground might swallow her up, but to her surprise Lord Belphege said unexpectedly, "Sarah is quite right. I should explain myself better. My sister Catherine, Miss Sinclair, is reckoned quite respectable, though I don't know about God-fearing. Her husband, I must admit, is neither respectable nor God-fearing, since he is that William Fulton whom we observed with his *amie* at the opera. But that does not signify. You will not meet him. My sister keeps house lavishly in Portman Square, and he keeps his actress in cosy rooms off Pall Mall and spends the larger part of his time there."

"I'm sorry," Aurelia said soberly.

"What about?"

"That your sister and her husband don't agree. It was embarrassing for you and Julia to have me see your brother-in-law in such circumstances at the opera."

"It did not embarrass me and it only infuriated Julia. Besides, I did not say that Kate and William don't agree—they agree perfectly. They agree to keep out of each other's way. I assure you, they are a happy pair."

"You ought not to speak so lightly of it!" Aurelia said severely.

"I am quite serious. I can honestly say that I have never heard either Catherine or William speak a harsh word to or about each other. Of how many couples, living in domestic partnership under the same roof, can you say that?"

"Not many, I suppose!" retorted Aurelia. "But I don't account it a fault if husband and wife squabble a little. If they never fell out they'd be a couple of vegetables."

"Possibly!" he said, laughing. "You are quite probably right. Come to that, my brother-in-law does put one in mind of a vegetable; a turnip, I think! Anyhow, although he will not be present on Tuesday, Catherine and her friends will be, and anxious to meet you."

Aurelia drew a little circle in the dust with the point of her parasol. "You know, Lord Belphege," she said meekly, "I do appreciate the trouble you are taking to introduce me into polite society. After all, it was to your mother I wrote for help, not to you."

"It is my pleasure, Miss Sinclair," he replied courteously with a bow.

"But I can't help wondering," continued Aurelia with a demure glance up at him, "just why you are putting yourself to so much inconvenience on my account."

"Oh, I have my reasons, Aurel—Miss Sinclair!"

"That, sir, is what I suspect! Might I know your reasons?"

"All in good time," he promised her, twinkling at her infuriatingly from under his thick black brows.

"*Now* would be a good time!" Aurelia insisted firmly.

"No, it wouldn't. There are too many people about." He glanced around them as he spoke and his expression sharpened and he said, "Hullo, this is a coincidence! Here comes someone else I want you to meet."

Aurelia turned in the direction he indicated and to her surprise saw approaching them Julia's escort. Of Julia there was no sign. The couple had presumably parted, leaving each to make a separate way out of the Park to their respective homes.

The man stopped short when he saw Harry and said, "Oh, Harry!" in rather a lame voice, adding, "I didn't know you were in the Park this morning," in a tone of voice that rather indicated that if he had known, he would have taken care to be elsewhere. He looked rather confused and distinctly unhappy.

"Everyone is in the Park this morning!" remarked Lord Belphege enigmatically. "Miss Sinclair, I wanted to present this gentleman to you at my mother's house, but unfortunately he left early before I could do so. Allow me to present to you now Mr. Antony Helliwell. His family also has connections with Jamaica."

Aurelia's face drained of colour and she stared at Antony like one who has seen a ghost. "Helliwell?" she whispered.

Behind her, Sarah gave a heart-rending groan and wailed, "There! Didn't I just tell 'ee, Miss Aury? Didn't I warn 'ee?"

Aurelia pulled herself together and snapped, "Be quiet, Sarah! Whatever can you mean? I . . . I am pleased to make your acquaintance, Mr. Helliwell."

Lord Belphege was watching with a frown and Antony

Helliwell, looking puzzled, returned the courtesy a little hesitantly, glancing at Harry for guidance.

"Are you all right, Aurelia?" Lord Belphege asked quietly. "You look a little pale."

"I am quite all right, sir, thank you!" she returned briskly. "But I really must beg of you both, gentlemen, to excuse me. I must be going. Come along, Sarah!"

Sarah gave Antony a look which might have been reserved for one who had just risen from the infernal regions, equipped with tail and trident. Then she scurried after Aurelia.

"Well, I didn't quite expect that!" said Harry slowly. "I'm sorry, Tony, embarrassing for you."

"I don't understand," said the honest Mr. Helliwell, quite bewildered. "I was never handsome, but I've never frightened a girl nearly into a faint before, just by looking at her!"

"Don't worry, Tony," Harry said thoughtfully. "It wasn't your looks, it was your name. Your face meant nothing to her. I don't mean that disrespectfully, my dear chap! But it wasn't until she heard your name that she took fright. Tell me, have you heard from your father yet?"

"Not yet," said Mr. Helliwell, "but I hope I do soon. I admit I'm now as curious as you are, Harry, to know something about Miss Sinclair!"

CHAPTER
FIVE

THE Polite World was a small and closed community. This much Aurelia had quickly discovered. She fully understood, therefore, the social value to her of Harry's invitation. What she could not fathom out, despite much racking of her brains, was the intention behind it. For the one thing Lord Belphege did not have in mind was the simple promotion of Miss Sinclair's social career, and Miss Sinclair knew it.

"He is up to some trick!" she told her mirror. "But he will find I am not a ninny. Does he think I am to be so flattered by his attentions that I will not question his motives? Ha!" Her reflection nodded sternly back at her. "We shall see, sir, we shall see!"

Thus determined, Aurelia, dressed in a trim walking-dress with matching spencer and a jaunty bonnet with a curled feather bobbing atop it, left Sarah to the inevitable pile of mending and set off for her milliner. She had ordered a bonnet and was horribly afraid that the cost of it was going to prove exorbitant. However, she needed it and the money must be found. Secretly she was beginning to worry that she would not find a suitable partner for her schemes in time—in time, that was, before her money ran out. She could not live in London indefinitely, pursuing the social round. Besides, apart from the cost of it all, people might start any day to ask questions about her family and the now celebrated sugar estate in Jamaica. And there were other matters which Aurelia had prudently not mentioned to Captain Foote.

At the door of the milliner's she almost collided with a couple coming out, so absorbed was she in her own difficulties.

"Beg pardon ma'am!" said the gentleman, raising his hat.

Aurelia blinked and stared at him. It was unmistakably the William Fulton who was brother-in-law, and an erring one, to Julia and Harry. Worse, he had his mistress on his arm.

"My fault, sir," stammered Aurelia. "I was not looking where I was going!"

She felt herself colouring. She was sure he had recognised her and also that he knew she had recognised him. He was staring at her very boldly and in a manner for which she did not care. Viewed at closer hand he seemed younger than at the opera and was still a fine-looking man, though the signs of drink and dissipation were writ clear on his features and had ruined what would otherwise have been a handsome countenance. His complexion had an unhealthy pallor, as if it seldom saw the light of day and its owner was accustomed to move about only by candlelight. Further evidence of the hours he kept was supplied by the shadows under his eyes and the pouched, drooping eyelids. From beneath these eyelids his eyes now ran over her figure insolently, making no pretence. Aurelia had the awful feeling that somehow his gaze had the power of stripping her naked. She felt her face burning and she wanted nothing so much as to run away.

Then he spoke. "I am the one to apologise, ma'am, for I certainly cannot say I did not notice *you*! Such a thing would be impossible." He bowed to accompany his tarnished gallantry.

"Um. . ." muttered Aurelia, trying to pass him by and enter the shop.

"Really, Billy!" the damsel on his arm said sharply. "Do come along! We don't have all day for you to stand about ogling every little Miss who passes by!"

This speech dealt summarily with Aurelia's unwonted feelings of cowardice and aroused her fighting spirit. She stared the lady firmly in the eye and had the satisfaction of seeing her opponent, after a second, quail before that militant gaze and look rather sheepishly down at the pavement.

"It is not my intention, madam," said Aurelia grandly, "to inconvenience you, nor to take up any of your valuable time! I only wish to call on the milliner. Please walk on."

"Come along, Billy, at once!" snapped the other, scarlet with rage. She tugged at Fulton's arm and dragged him off towards a waiting carriage.

"Damn you, Nancy," he could be heard protesting as his forceful paramour bundled him into the carriage, "can't you mind your tongue in public?"

"I'll mind my tongue, sir, when you mind your gaze," was the tart reply.

By now Aurelia was dying to meet Mr. Fulton's wife that evening. However, more immediate matters claimed her attention just now. She entered the milliner's premises and closed the door carefully. Despite her care, the bell above the door jangled shrilly and immediately, summoned by its call, a very thin young woman appeared from behind a curtain. "Like a djinn," thought Aurelia.

"Good morning, madam," said the thin female ingratiatingly. "May I be of service?"

"I would like to see Madame Spinelli," Aurelia told her.

"Perhaps you'd like to take a seat, madam?" The minion offered her a chair. "I'll tell Madame Spinelli directly. What name, please, madam?"

"Sinclair," Aurelia said.

A flicker of intelligence gleamed briefly in the thin young woman's lack-lustre eyes. "Yes, madam," she murmured and withdrew behind the curtain.

Aurelia glanced around the little shop. Two bonnets, both of the first elegance and no doubt correspondingly highly priced, perched on stands on the counter. They were the only articles of millinery to be seen. Madame Spinelli did not cater for the vulgar public. She created to order. Aurelia tried to relax and look at ease. She had come with the intention of settling her account, as well as to see the bonnet she had ordered. After the milliner's she had to proceed to the dressmaker, there to pay for the gold organdie and to enquire about the cost of two new walking-out dresses she needed. At this rate she soon would not even have the return fare to Jamaica should she need it.

A door opened somewhere in the back of the shop and a burst of female chatter indicated it was that of Madame Spinelli's workroom. The door was shut and the babble cut off. The curtain was whisked aside and the milliner bounced energetically into the shop in a flurry of black taffeta, followed by the thin young woman, who was carrying a large hat-box.

"Dear Miss Sinclair!" cried Madame Spinelli effusively. "Only yesterday I said to my girls, the bonnet for Miss Sinclair must be finished immediately! And, behold, the bonnet!" She flung a hand dramatically towards the thin girl who rushed forward with the hat-box, opened it, and withdrew Aurelia's bonnet with a flourish.

Aurelia, overcome by the unexpected warmth of the welcome, was a little bemused but still able to see that the bonnet was beautifully made.

"You like it, yes?" crowed Madame Spinelli. "You will try it on? Jennings, the mirror!"

Jennings—the thin girl—set down the bonnet and produced a mirror by some sleight-of-hand from below the counter. Madame Spinelli herself set the bonnet on Miss Sinclair's head.

"Charming! Charming! Is it not charming, Jennings?" Jennings agreed breathlessly that it was.

Aurelia turned her head from side to side and looked at the reflection in the mirror. "It's very nice," she said. "In fact, it's beautiful, Madame Spinelli."

"Ah, dear signorina!" cried the milliner. "But to make for such a pretty head is a pleasure indeed!"

The seed of doubt which had been planted in Aurelia's mind by the effusive welcome was now turning to cold suspicion. Madame Spinelli's manner was such as must be reserved for very favoured, and very rich, customers. Yet, when Aurelia had come to order the bonnet originally the milliner's manner had been, to put it mildly, cool. What had caused this change? Cautiously Aurelia broached the subject of the bill.

"Oh, but you need not pay *now*!" cried the milliner. "We can place it upon your account. If you are satisfied, perhaps you will do us the honour of allowing us to create for you again, Signorina Sinclair?"

Aurelia found herself giving Madame Spinelli the honour of an order for a garden hat in Italian straw. Madame Spinelli positively radiated delight. Aurelia, puzzled and not a little alarmed, was bowed out of the shop with ceremony. Promises to send the finished bonnet to Aurelia's lodgings directly floated out behind her.

Quite at a loss, Aurelia proceeded to Madame Baraud, the dressmaker. On her last visit hints had been dropped that an early settlement of the bill for the gold organdie would be appreciated.

"But Mademoiselle need not pay immediately!" crooned the dressmaker. "We shall put it on Mademoiselle's personal account! If I might show Mademoiselle the new muslins which have just come in? Or this blue silk? As soon as I saw this silk I thought of *you*, dear Mademoiselle Sinclair!" She pressed dress patterns and sample swatches of material for the walking-out dresses on Aurelia.

Aurelia left the dressmaker's as bewildered as she had been on leaving the milliner's. She herself had done nothing to indicate to these ladies that here was a prized new customer. Indeed, she had been careful only to order such articles as were well within her purse, and it had been her concern for the price of every yard of satin ribbon which had led to her original cool reception in these establishments. But now . . .

Luckily, she was not able to hear Madame Baraud's observations after her departure.

"*Tiens*, but that little one is a strange child! So lovely and yet so cautious! The first time she came here she asked the price of everything, but everything! Never did I think that her credit would be guaranteed by an English milord, no less!"

"Well, she's immensely pretty," said her chief henchwoman enviously. "I'm not surprised she's aimed high for a protector!"

"Ah," Madame Baraud lowered her voice to a conspiratorial whisper. "It is true that he wishes his interest to be kept secret, but that does not mean that the affair is altogether dishonourable, no, no! That little one, she is no lightskirt. Do I not see these girls with their gentlemen protectors? No, no, Miss Sinclair is no mistress in keeping. Only imagine if the noble gentleman plans to *marry* her, eh? Luisa Spinelli tells me he has guaranteed her credit there, too! If we are a little nice to her now, and one day she is milady, ah, then we have gained a good customer, I think!"

Of Lady Belphege's eight children, Aurelia had only met Harry and Julia. It was natural, then, that she should imagine their sister Catherine as something of a cross between these two. In this she was not so very far wrong, at least in as far as physical resemblance was concerned. The Honourable Mrs. Fulton was slightly above middle height and of sturdy build. She had pretty fair hair and a smooth, creamy skin very faintly dotted with pale brown freckles which a layer of powder tried hard to disguise. She moved slowly and with a curious dreamy air of abstraction, as if hers were not earthly cares. She also had a trick of fixing her gaze on some vague point above the head or over the shoulder of the person to whom she was speaking, as if she were not quite aware of that person's presence.

This habit of not looking a person in the eye was, Aurelia decided quickly, like the air of dreamy abstraction, a contrived mannerism. This very attractive woman was absolutely aware of everything—and everyone—about her. She took Aurelia's hand limply in hers and with her eye fixed, it seemed, on the lower pendant of the crystal chandelier hanging from the ornate painted ceiling, murmured, "So nice to meet you, Miss Sinclair. . . . Harry has told me so much. . ." Then, before Aurelia had a chance to open her mouth to reply, Catherine turned to her brother and, as if Aurelia had somehow completely disappeared, enquired absently, "How are you, Harry?"

Aurelia's hackles rose. She knew when she had been snubbed, even when it had been done as elegantly as this!

"Very well, Kate!" returned Lord Belphege, the light of battle glinting for an instant in his eye. "And how are my nephews? Kate here has a pair of boisterous youngsters, Aurelia."

Aurelia could not help looking a little surprised. From

what she had learned of the Fultons' domestic arrangements, it seemed astonishing that the couple had produced one, let alone two, offspring.

Catherine looked faintly disconcerted before her
brother's direct gaze. "Oh, the boys are quite well,
Harry. They're up in the nursery. . . ." She gestured
vaguely towards the ceiling, as if the nursery were to be
found somewhere in the upper reaches of the house, but
she was not quite sure where.

"I should like to meet your little boys," Aurelia said
brightly. "I like children."

Catherine, forced to pay direct attention to her guest,
brought her gaze down from the ceiling and fixed it
momentarily on Aurelia. She had eyes as bright and
sharp as a pair of blue diamonds. "How nice. . ." she
said, and her lips half-formed a smile.

It was not much of a smile, but it sufficed to let Aurelia
glimpse sound but decidedly crooked teeth. "She
doesn't smile because of her teeth," thought Aurelia
triumphantly. Now that she had surprised this little
secret in her hostess she no longer felt ill at ease, and
fairly beamed at Catherine in a manner which Sarah
would have declared brazen.

"Don't underestimate Kate, she's devoted to her
brats!" Harry whispered in Aurelia's ear as he led her
away. "And she is quite a force in Society. If Kate speaks
well of you, a hundred doors will open to you. Well, a
dozen, anyway."

Aurelia doubted that Catherine would speak well of
her, but then she remembered that the lady spoke well of
her estranged husband, so possibly the Honourable Mrs.
Fulton's Likes and Dislikes were more complex than
other peoples'.

"To business!" thought Aurelia severely. "I am not
here to amuse myself." Surreptitiously she began to
study the other guests. One thing they all seemed to have

in common—money. That was obvious from their
general appearance and manner of speech. Whether any
one of them could be persuaded to invest some of his
surplus wealth in a run-down Jamaican sugar estate was
another matter, and one to which Aurelia now turned
her attention.

The buzz of conversation during the first course of
the dinner gave her the opportunity to study them all
individually, as she sampled the stewed mushrooms and
toyed with the bombarded veal. There was a plump little
man, his hands loaded with rings, who could be a distinct
possibility. There was a tall, angular lady wearing beautiful pearls who would be unlikely to so much as listen to
Aurelia's ideas. A peer of the realm ate in gloomy
silence whilst a florid lady beside him chattered inces-
santly. Either of them might bear investigation.

The first course was carried away by footmen in
splendid livery, and the many dishes comprising the
second course brought in. The huge oval table was now
dominated by a wonderful pudding veiled in spun sugar
net, a triumph of culinary skills.

"I recognise the hand of Marcel," observed Harry to
Aurelia. "I see he still presides over Kate's kitchen.
I'm sure he is the last member of her staff she would
turn away. Half her guests come for Marcel's cooking."

Aurelia wondered vaguely why Catherine should turn
off any of her staff. Their hostess, who had eaten heartily
of all fifteen dishes of the first course, could now be
heard declaring that she never ate *anything* at the second
course but a little of the jelly, prettily coloured green
with spinach juice and flavoured with liqueur. Her cheeks
were slightly flushed and she had grown almost
animated. She was seated next to a gentleman of
academic mien who also appeared to appreciate a good
dinner, for he was busily wiping his chin free of gravy

while expounding on the movement of the stars. Occasionally he and their hostess exchanged coy glances which had nothing to do with heavenly bodies.

"Tch!" thought Aurelia, who by now had learned to recognise the signs which hinted at intrigues of an amorous nature. Her eye ran along the other faces round the table, wondering if any one of them would serve the purpose which had brought her to London. Suddenly she looked up and caught Harry's eye on her. He looked amused. She had a dreadful feeling that he knew what she was about and could read her mind as easily as a book.

"How do you find all these people?" he whispered to her.

"Very pleasant," Aurelia returned promptly.

"Not a trifle dull?"

"Well, perhaps I don't share all their interests," was the diplomatic reply.

"But they all share a common interest," he remarked. "They are all very interested in money. Naturally they would scorn the sordid means by which it is obtained, trade for instance. But they are not loath to accumulate it, all the same, nor to spend it. It is their devouring passion. How about you, Aurelia?"

Aurelia turned pale and whispered angrily, "If I am interested in money, it's not for the reason you suppose! I would not waste wealth on frivolities, but use it for practical projects!"

"Ah!" he said. He looked satisfied and sat back and smiled at her in a way that Aurelia could only describe as smug.

What she might have replied was not to be known. Unexpectedly the gloomy peer who had been the prisoner of the chattering lady, leaned across the table and, fixing Aurelia with a bloodshot eye, bellowed, "Jamaica, is it, m'dear?"

Aurelia was too startled to reply.

"Miss Sinclair is from Jamaica," Harry said smoothly.

"Antigua," said the other briefly.

"No, sir, Jamaica," Aurelia protested.

He gave her a look which suggested he thought her a trifle simple. "*I* own land in Antigua!" he said.

Aurelia blushed. "Oh, I see. Do you?"

"Never been there," he said, "too dashed warm. Too warm by far, eh, Miss Simpson?"

"Sinclair!" Aurelia said a little desperately.

"Too warm!" he insisted, and fell back into his previous gloomy silence.

Aurelia crossed him off her list. No use approaching him with details of failing sugar estates. He would only blame it all on the heat.

"I don't think so, either," Harry said pleasantly.

Aurelia almost jumped out of her seat. "I don't understand you!" she gasped hastily.

"I meant I don't think his conversation is very entertaining. That seemed to be your opinion, too," Harry supplied, smiling kindly at her.

For the rest of the evening Aurelia could not rid herself of the uncomfortable feeling that her every word, movement and expression were observed by Lord Belphege. Even when he was talking to other people it seemed as if his eyes were upon her and there was something in those eyes which Aurelia did not quite understand.

One thing was quite clear, however. She would have to find a way, somehow or other, to end her acquaintance with Lord Belphege. He was presumptuous, mocking and dangerous to her plans. It was a pity to be forced to turn her back on the one door Society had opened to her, but it couldn't be helped. She could not afford to take risks. Harry was playing with her like a cat with a mouse, but eventually he would tire of the game

. . . and when that happened the cat inevitably ate its plaything. Yes, Harry could ruin everything!

By a stroke of irony, on the selfsame evening as Aurelia took her stern decision to end her acquaintance with Harry, someone else was plotting to achieve the same purpose, namely to drive a wedge in the blossoming friendship of Lord Belphege and Miss Aurelia Sinclair.

"And, do you know, Antony?" demanded Julia with sweeping rhetoric, "can you just imagine it? He has actually taken that girl to my sister's—Catherine's—house this evening!"

Mr. Helliwell, sitting on the very edge of his chair and half preoccupied with listening for Lady Belphege's approach, looked cautious and murmured, "Why, is that so very bad?"

"Bad? It is disastrous!" cried Julia, starting back in horror.

There was a distant sound as of a door closing and her visitor half rose to his feet. "Upon my soul, Julia, I don't feel easy. Suppose your mother were to discover me here?"

"Oh, for goodness' sake, Antony, do sit down! Mother has gone to bed. I've told you that at least a dozen times. She always retires early when she has no social engagement."

"I thought I heard a door. . ." muttered her swain, not convinced and glancing apprehensively all around the room and up at the ceiling, as if he expected Lady Belphege to descend in a cardboard chariot like the *deus ex machina* of a stage play.

"It will be the servants tidying up!" said Julia, brushing aside his fears. "Antony, I asked you most particularly to come this evening to discuss my brother and Miss Sinclair, and I do not believe you have heard one word in three that I have said."

"Yes, I have!" he defended himself. "But I don't like sneaking in and out of the place unbeknown to your mother. I know she don't care for me—she makes it plain enough." He fidgeted uncomfortably on his chair and burst out, "Besides, Julia, to be honest it don't seem right to be discussing Harry's affairs behind his back like this."

"I am not discussing Harry's affairs behind his back!" returned Julia with dignity. "I am discussing what may be done on Harry's behalf. Really, Antony, you profess to be a friend of Harry's. Don't you care that he is being deceived by that adventuress?"

"Now just hold on one moment, Julia!" said Mr. Helliwell firmly. "In the first place it would be a difficult thing for anyone to deceive Harry for very long. Harry is as shrewd a man as I know. Secondly, you don't know that she's an adventuress. She may well be a very respectable young woman."

"Oh, pshaw!" exclaimed Julia, too irritated to find words for the moment.

"You may pooh-pooh anything I say, my dear," he said mildly, "but we have no proof."

"Then we must acquire some proof!" Julia urged him, regaining speech. That is where you can help, Antony."

"I, ma'am?" He glanced towards the door again as if by now he was beginning to hope that Lady Belphege, garbed like Lady Macbeth in night attire and carrying a candle, would burst in upon them and order him to leave her house.

"You, Antony. Because you have connections in Jamaica and we can use them to make inquiries about her."

"Ah!" said Mr. Helliwell, opening and closing his mouth like a stranded trout.

"Why not?" cried Julia, misunderstanding his signs of distress. "You must write to Jamaica straight away,

Antony, and find out everything you can about her, her family, her home, everything!"

There was a silence. "Are you quite sure you haven't spoken to Harry?" he asked her, adding immediately, "No, of course you have not, or you wouldn't have made that suggestion."

Julia, like her mother, was quick to catch disguised references in casual words. "What do you mean? Why do you say that?"

Mr Helliwell thumped one fist unhappily into the palm of the other hand two or three times and replied unhappily, "Damn it, Julia, you place me in the devil of a spot! For you oblige me to break a confidence. Well, not exactly a confidence, but to speak to you of a matter which Harry might wish kept private."

"Go on!" ordered Julia ominously.

"Well, to tell the truth, my dear," he continued, growing visibly more wretched as he spoke, "Harry has asked me to do the very same thing!"

The effect of his words on the lady was most gratifying. Julia's mouth fell open and it was some moments before she summoned enough presence of mind to whisper, "Harry did? Asked you to enquire about Miss Sinclair?"

He nodded. "Wants to know all about her, family, property, everything."

"Then his intentions must be serious!" Julia cried dramatically. "He is thinking of marriage! It must be stopped!"

"You leap to conclusions, Julia," argued Mr. Helliwell. "Perhaps he too has his suspicions."

"At any rate, we shall know sooner than I anticipated," said Julia in a businesslike manner, "for the matter is already set in hand. You *have* written, I take it?"

"To my father. He will write, or has probably written

by now, to Jamaica and our agent. If there is anything, good or bad, to be known about Miss Sinclair, my dear, we shall know it. But it takes a little time for a letter to reach Jamaica and a reply to come back."

"You can have no idea," Julia told him earnestly, "how much this sets my mind at rest."

A demon took possession of Mr. Helliwell. "He might get married before a letter comes," he pointed out.

Julia fell back in her chair and he leapt up in alarm, fearing that she was about to faint. But Julia was made of sterner material and not given to swooning away on the carpet, even when smitten with such a disastrous notion as this. "That must not happen!" she hissed at him between clenched teeth. "I will prevent it by any means."

"I don't suppose it will," he hastened to assure her. "If Harry asked me to get certain information then he won't act before he has it."

But Julia was looking thoughtful. She stood up and walked slowly to a nearby mirror and looked appraisingly at her own image. "Miss Sinclair is very pretty, don't you think?" she asked her visitor in a matter-of-fact way. "Any man would be attracted to her."

"Some would think so, I suppose," he said diplomatically. "I don't care for frills and furbelows myself. I'm a plain man and she would be too much of a high-stepper for me."

Julia smiled and turned to face him. "I do envy her sometimes," she admitted. She sounded embarrassed by the admission.

He was genuinely surprised. "Whatever for?"

"Because she is pretty and vivacious and knows how to dress. Miss Sinclair would not be misled into wearing a gown like this one, which did not suit her."

He was a true lover. "I have been wanting to tell you, Julia m'dear, that I find that gown very fetching on you, my word of honour I do!" He came over to her and took her hand awkwardly. "See here, Julia, you know I would not have you any different to the way you are. Miss Sinclair may do very well for the Harrys of the world, but you are the one for me and always will be!"

"Oh, Antony," said Julia, pressing his hand. "I really believe you are the finest man I have ever met."

"Finer than Harry?" he asked with a touch of humour.

"Harry is my brother. One cannot include him. You have made me very happy, Antony. You do not know how much."

"We should be a good deal happier if we could be married and you could be away from here. What is the use of my creeping around the place like a sneakthief? Sooner or later we must tell Harry. . . and your mother!"

"Mother would never permit me to leave her or to marry you or anyone!" Julia retorted bitterly. "And Harry has his head full of Aurelia and is so used to my being an old maid that I dare say if I told him I wished to be married, he'd fall off his chair laughing. It's no good, Antony, I am over thirty and I do not have the courage of a young girl. If I were twenty I'd tell you to put a ladder up to my window and we would be away to Gretna Green and be married over the anvil. But not now."

"Creeping about, with or without a ladder under my arm, isn't in my line," he said a little grumpily. "Damn it, Julia, I know I'm no catch and your mother thinks me an upstart—and I dare say Harry would not think me good enough to marry into a family of title—but we are a respectable family with nothing to be ashamed of. It does not seem fair that a woman old enough to know her own mind and a man of thirty-five who is perfectly convinced he has found the wife for him, cannot be married because of a set of rules contrived by Society and the whims of a bad-tempered old lady! Beg pardon, my dear, I should not speak of your mother so, but I can't help it."

Mention the spirits and they appear. Mr. Helliwell should have thought of that. There was a scuttling outside the door which was pushed open to admit the frightened face of Julia's maid, who uttered a single electrifying sentence, "Lady Belphege is coming downstairs!"

There was instant chaos. Mr. Helliwell dropped Julia's hand and darted a hunted glance around him, apparently undecided whether to hide behind the long-case clock or dive beneath the sofa. Julia ran towards the door and, pushing the terrified maid ahead of her, could be heard urging, "Delay her! Delay her!"

"I can't, madam!" wailed the maid.

Julia reappeared, breathless. "Antony, quick! You must slip out before she comes!"

"Julia!" came a familiar imperious voice. "Where are you? I have mislaid that ridiculous reading-glass. Where is it?"

"She would lose it now!" exclaimed Julia, exasperated. "Normally she refuses to use it, now she must have it! I'll have to go and help her, Antony, you must leave."

"How?" he demanded. "Lady Belphege is coming down the stairs. How am I to get across the hall?"

It could not be done and Julia saw the impossibility. "Then you must go out of the window!" she declared and running to the nearest window, pulled back the curtains and pushed up the sash. "Come along!" she encouraged him. "We are on the ground floor."

"It's a wonder I'm not expected to leap out from a storey up!" he muttered rebelliously as he swung his legs over the sill. "Upon my word, I never felt so ridiculous.

If the Watch should see me and raise a hue and cry I'd not be surprised."

But his love was too anxious to have him gone to heed his complaints. Energetically she gave him a hearty shove, slammed down the window as he disappeared from view, and dragged the curtains closed. As she turned to face the door she heard a muffled yelp from outside, where Mr. Helliwell had landed on his knees in a small bed of rose bushes.

"Good heavens, girl!" declared Lady Belphege, coming into the room. "Why is there such a draught in here, and why are you standing to attention like that?" She looked about her peevishly. "I left the reading-glass in here, I am sure of it."

"Could you not have sent Addams down for it?" Julia asked her crossly. Addams was Lady Belphege's long-suffering maid.

"I sent Addams to bed," said her ladyship irritably. "Stop blithering, Julia, and help me look. Ah, yes, there it is!" She gestured with her stick toward a small table on which, sure enough, lay the reading-glass, the cause of so much disturbance.

She made a stately return to her bedchamber, despite her nightcap being askew, followed by Julia with the candle and reading glass. Once there, Lady Belphege sat down on the edge of her bed and demanded, "Is my cap crooked? Put it straight!"

Julia obediently set the cap straight and retied the ribbons under her mother's chin. The reason for Lady Belphege's concern was obvious and near at hand. On a wooden wigstand beside the bed stood the head of shining silver curls so admired by Aurelia. Lady Belphege was quite bald.

CHAPTER
SIX

FOR the next few days Aurelia saw and heard nothing from Harry, or any other member of his family, and true to her resolve, she studiously avoided calling on Lady Belphege or going anywhere where a member of the family might be found. Then, one morning, Sarah appeared with a letter in her hand which she held out gingerly towards Aurelia, as if it might burst into flames.

"I don't like the look of this, Miss Aury."

"Who brought it?" asked Aurelia, taking the little package and breaking the seal.

"One of they fancy footmen. Don't you open it, that's my advice. Burn 'un, I say."

"Why should I burn it when I don't know what it says or who sent it? Anyway, I've broken the seal."

"It's got a bad feeling to it," Sarah said glumly.

"Nonsense!" said Aurelia, trying not to think that Sarah was all too often right. She opened the letter and smoothed it out flat. It was from Julia. She was sorry Miss Sinclair had not called recently and hoped Miss Sinclair was not indisposed. She would be greatly obliged if Miss Sinclair would call to see her, if possible that afternoon.

Aurelia read the letter carefully twice. Julia definitely said call on *her*, and not on Lady Belphege. It seemed very odd. Aurelia pursed her lips and drummed her fingertips on the table-top. She did not care for this letter. She was beginning to share Sarah's feelings of foreboding. Julia quite patently did not like her; it was hard to imagine why she should want to see her, and apparently on private business.

Sarah, who had had little schooling, was painstakingly deciphering the letter over Aurelia's shoulder and said now, "Don't you go, my lovely. You write and tell her you're proper indisposed and can't go nowhere."

"I have to go, Sarah. It would look so odd if I didn't."

Nevertheless, despite her decision to go, Aurelia did not intend to appear before Julia as if answering a summons, so she wrote a polite reply explaining that she was quite unable to come that afternoon, owing to a prior engagement. She would, however, call the next day.

She did not feel very happy the next afternoon as she pulled at the doorbell. The butler said she was expected and would she please come up straight away. He led Aurelia through the hall and up the stairs at such a brisk pace that it was quite obvious he had received instructions to let no one see Miss Sinclair. On the first floor she was shown into a small neat room which she realised must be Julia's private sitting-room.

Julia herself came to greet her. She looked a little tidier than usual. Her frizzy hair was secured by a bandeau and fluffed out attractively behind the band in a kind of halo about her head. She wore quite a pretty cherry-striped gown and it occurred to Aurelia that Julia had made a great effort to look her best. It was all very curious.

"You know my sister Catherine, I believe?" Julia said in a hurried way, as if anxious to have the preliminaries over and done with.

Aurelia had seen Catherine, who was seated by the fireplace, as soon as she had entered the room, but as Catherine had given no sign of recognition, Aurelia only now bowed slightly to the lady and said, "Yes, I do."

Catherine smiled vaguely at her, as usual contriving

not to open her lips. "So nice. . ." she said. She was
beautifully dressed. Her bonnet alone must have cost
the price of Aurelia's shawl and bonnet together, and
her gloves and Norwich lace shawl looked brand new.
Her gown was pale pink, a colour, Aurelia thought
unkindly, which was a little young for the wearer, as was
the style of the gown itself. But the overall effect was
striking, to say the least. Catherine was a very handsome
woman.

"Catherine and I," said Julia, who appeared to be the
appointed spokeswoman, "are really very grateful to
you for giving us your time, Miss Sinclair, and we do
hope that you will not take anything we say amiss. Please
sit down."

"I should like to hear what it is you have to say first,"
said Aurelia candidly as she sat down, "before I pass
judgement on it. How may I help you both?" Faintly she
emphasised the word 'both'. She did not like being out-
numbered two to one, and had the feeling that Julia had
not played quite fair in not telling her that both sisters
would be there to greet her.

Julia glanced at her sister as Aurelia finished speaking, but Catherine's gaze was fixed on the opposite
wall.

"Miss Sinclair, Catherine and I, as you probably
know, have five other sisters, but only one brother." She
paused, but as Aurelia said nothing, continued, "You
will understand that our brother Harry's actions are of
some concern to us."

Aurelia was at a loss but did not show it. "I understand, I suppose, but don't see how Lord Belphege's
actions can concern me," was her reply.

"Harry. . . Harry is sometimes impulsive. Nor is he
immune to female attractions. You are very pretty, Miss
Sinclair." Julia's face grew very red as she said this.

An incredible idea was slowly forming in Aurelia's

brain. Surely this mousy creature and her pretty doll of a sister didn't think . . .

"Julia is trying to say," said Catherine Fulton unexpectedly, "that we should not like our brother Harry to fall in love with you, Miss Sinclair."

Shattered, Aurelia snapped, "I should think that highly unlikely, ma'am."

Catherine brought her gaze down from the wall and fixed it on Aurelia, who was once more struck by how sharp and bright her eyes were. "Come, my dear," said Catherine smoothly, "you cannot be so naïve! You must know Harry is very interested in you. My dear child, he doesn't bring young ladies to my house every night of the week. Besides, others have noticed it too. Gussie Foote is spreading the notion all over Town."

"Oh, dear, kind Gussie!" Aurelia moaned inwardly, "how could you?" Outwardly she preserved her calm and, more to gain time than anything else, demanded, "May I ask whether you are speaking entirely on your own behalf, or on that of Lady Belphege?" It was a shot in the dark but a lucky one. Both sisters immediately looked very uncomfortable.

"My mother is very elderly," Julia said at last. "We naturally don't wish to trouble her with this. She is devoted to Harry and would be most upset."

"You flatter me," Aurelia said grimly.

"My dear Miss Sinclair," said Catherine amiably, "we *do* flatter you! You are the first young woman who has really succeeded in capturing Harry's attention to the extent that people are beginning to gossip about a possible engagement. That, I assure you, is no mean feat. You are obviously a young woman of outstanding attractions and qualities. Indeed, as soon as I set eyes upon you, I saw that you were an exceptional young person and that you will no doubt one day make a brilliant match! So you see, my dear, we do not mean to criticise

you personally in any way. But you must realise that a
match between you and Harry would be out of the
question." Her voice hardened slightly, and the glitter of
the sharp blue eyes belied the gracious manner and
persuasive charm of her speech.

Aurelia, in no way deceived, stood up and mustered
every ounce of dignity. "Firstly," she said, "such a
match *is* out of the question, if only for the reason that I
would never wish it!"

Catherine looked faintly amused and Julia outraged.
Perhaps the idea that someone simply might not want
her beloved Harry had not occurred to her. Her sister,
accustomed to play a rôle continually herself, saw others
as acting too, and gave Aurelia a gentle nod of
encouragement.

"Secondly," continued Aurelia, riding roughshod
over both the amused nod and the expression of outrage,
"the pair of you seem very anxious to organise your
brother's life. It has certainly not been my impression
that he needs your help!"

Julia coloured angrily. "You may think us interfering
if you wish. . ."

"I do!" interrupted Aurelia promptly.

"Well, then," snapped Julia, "remember, please, that
we *will* interfere, very much so, if you attempt to ensnare
Harry!"

"You are a very silly woman," Aurelia said coldly.
"Good day to you. Both of you!"

Catherine smiled serenely. "Good day, Miss Sinclair.
So glad we understand one another!"

When Aurelia had swept out, the sisters looked at
each other.

"Julia, my dear, I fear you mishandled that interview," said Catherine in a tone of mild reproof.

"I?" cried Julia, incensed. "Much help you were, I
must say! Why you had to be flattering the girl and

spreading your words with sugar icing, I don't know. You may look as romantic and charming as you wish, it didn't fool Miss Sinclair, and it doesn't fool me! Your reasons for preventing Harry marrying that girl are as strong as mine."

"Dear Harry!" said Catherine kindly.

"Don't you 'dear Harry' me!" stormed Julia. "You don't care a fig for Harry! I do! I don't want him to marry that girl because I know in my bones she's an adventuress. *I* am thinking of Harry. You are thinking of yourself. Harry is very generous at picking up all those bills of yours that your own husband can't or won't pay!"

"Poor dear William!" observed his wife charitably.

"Poor dear William is rapidly ruining himself with his courtesan! Very soon she will have spent every penny he has and then what will you do, dear sister? Run to Harry? Dear, kind Harry? Well, if Harry has a wife— especially *that* wife—and a family of his own, then dear Harry might not be in a position to pay your bills as well as his own!"

"You are becoming hysterical, Julia," observed her sister. "And that does not help. Of course poor William is practically penniless. I shouldn't be surprised to see him gaoled for debt very soon. Therefore I do need Harry. I need him far more than you do, Julia. I have two sons to bring up, educate and establish. With what am I going to do it? Only with Harry's help. So you see, I have a great deal more at stake than you in this matter!" She rose elegantly to her feet and draped the Norwich shawl round her shoulders. "When does Helliwell hope to hear from his father?"

"Soon—and he will tell Harry straight away."

"And if he learns nothing detrimental to Miss Sinclair?"

"He must! I know she's a fraud. But I can't prove it. I will, though!"

"Let us hope you are right, Julia. For if you are wrong, and Harry learns what we have done this afternoon, then I fear he will be very angry and I do so hate unpleasant scenes." Catherine surveyed her sister thoughtfully. "You are much improved of late, Julia. You are dressing your hair quite prettily and choosing your gowns with more care. I am pleased to see it. You were looking such a scarecrow before."

"At least," countered Julia, "I don't dress myself up like a girl half my age!"

"Are you comparing me with Miss Sinclair, by any chance, my dear?" asked her sister, peering into the mirror and patting her curls.

"There is no comparison!" said Julia cruelly. "The girl is eighteen and looks it. You are thirty-four, the mother of two, and although you're a good-looking woman, even a pink dress doesn't take away sixteen years."

Not even this shattered Catherine's air of calm. "Really, Julia, I begin to fear you are, as Miss Sinclair said, a very silly woman," she said sweetly. "Now, do remember, my dear, to find out from Helliwell at the earliest possible moment anything he has learned. Try to persuade him to give you his information before he passes it to Harry. It is fortunate that you also thought to ask him. If Harry is in love with this girl, then he may be tempted to suppress any adverse information about her. We must make sure that every unfortunate fact about her is known! And do keep it all from Mother until we have proof."

"Mother is besotted with that girl!" raged Julia. "I always knew Mother to be difficult, but now I think age is affecting her judgement. She actually told me this morning that she would be very pleased if Harry did marry that girl! 'I think, upon reflection,' she said, 'that Miss Sinclair may prove very suitable after all!'"

It would be difficult to describe adequately the fury which burned in Aurelia's bosom as she left the sisters. But by the time she had reached her own little sitting-room she had calmed down a little and was only very angry. By the evening she had cooled down sufficiently to try and review the position objectively.

She was now placed in a very awkward situation. Her resolve to cut herself off from Harry, and from Lady Belphege, now appeared in a different light. If she ceased to call on Lady Belphege and to accept Harry's invitations—assuming that he would issue any more— then Julia and Catherine would take it for granted that they had successfully 'warned off' Miss Sinclair. Aurelia could picture them crowing delightedly together over her humiliation and congratulating each other on how clever they had been. No! Never! Aurelia gritted her teeth. On the other hand, if she continued to call on Lady Belphege as usual and made no change in her habits, then Julia and Catherine would consider that she had picked up the gauntlet they had flung down and would be more than ever convinced that she was setting her cap at their brother. And of all the most exquisite nonsense, that was the last refinement. That she, Aurelia Sinclair, would demean herself to beguile any man into marriage, and that Harry was witless idiot enough to let himself be beguiled, was ridiculous beyond belief. They must think Harry quite stupid, seethed Aurelia to herself. Unless Lord Belphege had made a life long habit of proposing to strange young women, she could not imagine why either sister had imagined it was his intention to propose to her.

"Keep frowning like that and the mark'll stay," warned Sarah.

Aurelia made a conscious effort to smooth her brow. "Yes, Sarah, I know."

"And I know I was right to try and stop you going over

there. I wish I had those two fine ladies here!" Sarah went on wrathfully. "They'd feel the edge of my tongue. Upsetting you like this. They don't have no call nor no right to do it!"

"Yes, they did upset me, Sarah. But it doesn't signify, for I mean to go on just as though I had not met with them today."

"Stands to reason, my lovely, if that Miss Julia is so thick and friendly with anyone by the name o' Helliwell, then she can't be any friend of yours."

"No. . ." Aurelia was staring thoughtfully into space. "I wonder how much she knows? I mean, could Helliwell have told her anything? Or would he know anything to tell? I wonder . . ."

"You should never have gone there!" repeated Sarah finally.

The next day nothing happened, other than that with a new dawn some sanity seemed to return to the world. The day following, Lord Belphege called in the afternoon and offered to take Aurelia for a drive. By now Aurelia had carefully prepared how she should receive him.

"Thank you," she said graciously. "I should love to come."

"Well, Aurelia?" he asked as they bowled merrily along. "What are your impressions of England now?"

"I can't say they have changed very much," she returned frankly. "Although I must say the weather has improved. When I first came it rained so, and there was such a terrible fog which lasted for two whole days! I couldn't set foot out of doors. I wonder you don't all succumb to pneumonia."

"We're a hardy lot. My mother suffers greatly in damp weather, as you can imagine, but it is remarkable how many of us survive our atrocious climate extremely well, and even grow to like it! I have known travellers return from the sunshine of Italy and comment that they missed the refreshing showers of rain which punctuate our English summer. You should come down to Eastfield, that's my country place, and see it in the summer, or better, in the spring! I don't believe you would find a prettier place anywhere, with all the buds bursting on the trees and the grass green and smooth as a carpet."

"I cannot imagine you in the country, Lord Belphege," Aurelia said slyly. "You seem so at home here, in Town."

"I am like the snail, Miss Sinclair. I can carry my home on my back! I am able to make myself comfortable almost anywhere, and I have been very few places which I have found really dull. There is always something to amuse one, or to intrigue one. . . or even to mystify one!" He gave her a wicked glance.

"Indeed, sir?" said Aurelia calmly, putting up her parasol against the watery sunshine.

"My dear Aurelia, you will forgive the suggestion, but I do think you should lower that pretty parasol, for we are coming to some trees and I should not like to think it would catch on any low branches," he advised her kindly.

Aurelia snapped the parasol shut in some irritation. "I'm sure I do not know why I put it up," she said crossly. "For, as I said, the weather is so overcast it is scarcely necessary."

"It is brightening. Look, you can see the sun up there," he pointed towards the clouds with his whip. "Put it in your diary! 'Dear Diary, today the sun shone on me while I was wearing my blue gown and pelisse and driving with Lord B—.' Though I should not tease you about it. Even Julia was complaining of aches and pains when I saw her this morning."

Was it by chance he mentioned his sister? "Did she? I am sorry."

"Yes," he said. "It's curious. Julia is never ill and the weather is not cold or wet, only a little dull. But she complained of stabbing pains in the back. I advised her to rest. My mother . . ." he broke off and then finished obscurely, " . . . my mother does not always realise how busy Julia's day is."

"I'm sure it is," thought Aurelia uncharitably. "What with running to meet Antony Helliwell in the park every morning, and then scampering home again before Lady Belphege finds out!"

"We have thoroughly discussed the weather," he said. "Do tell me, has nothing else in England impressed you?"

Aurelia had received a wealth of impressions of England but they were not all communicable to her companion, so she fixed her eyes on the pricked ears of the horse ahead and replied, "I enjoyed the opera. It was kind of you to take me."

He slowed the horse to a walk and said slowly and carefully, "Aurelia, I have something of a confession to make to you. I hope you will bear with me."

"Do you feel obliged to make it, sir?"

"Yes, I do. It concerns our first meeting. When I first saw you, I mean, at my mother's house, when you first called there—I was, well, frankly I was a little suspicious of your motives. Now, that is not the sort of thing I should be saying to you, because it was ungallant, unfounded and unworthy. I could, I suppose, excuse myself by saying that I was a little out of sorts that day and deuced foul-tempered. But it would be a poor excuse."

Aurelia, feeling about three inches high, gulped and whispered, "Please do not continue, sir!"

"Oh, but I wish to, and I must! You see, London is full of all kinds of people, and many of them are attracted to wealth and fashion for reasons which they would not always wish to have known openly."

Aurelia was scarlet and could say nothing.

"You are offended," he said, interpreting her silence as shock. "I am sorry. It pains me very much to confess that I ever doubted you. But I did. . . for a little while. You arrived so unexpectedly. Nobody knew you. You are, my dear, extremely pretty. However, my acquaintance with you since that first meeting has led me to believe I was wrong, and I apologise to you most humbly, Aurelia, for anything I may have thought then."

"Please don't," mumbled Aurelia.

"You are, Aurelia, quite the most remarkable young woman I have ever had the good fortune to meet. It is perhaps, too much to ask to be forgiven, but I do ask it. And if you can bring yourself to overlook my churlish doubts of you, then I hope you will see that my expressions of admiration are very deeply felt."

"Lord Belphege!" begged Aurelia. "Please don't distress yourself for anything you may have thought of me! And please do not continue in this fashion. It is not necessary."

He reined up the gig and turned to face her. "You cannot pretend to misunderstand me, Aurelia! I am sure that my deep interest in you has been apparent these last weeks, and you surely do not think that I am accustomed to unburden myself in this fashion to every girl I meet!"

"I do not think I misunderstand you, Lord Belphege," Aurelia interrupted hastily. "But please do not go on! This *is* a misunderstanding, but on your part, on everyone's part! Everyone seems to think that . . ." she trailed off miserably.

"Think what?"

"Well, they all seem to think that I . . . I have set my cap at you, Lord Belphege. That is not so."

"I know it isn't so," he said. "It is I who am pursuing you, if you like! And my name is Harry."

"Then, Lord Belphege . . ."

"Harry!"

"I'm sorry, then, Harry, you must know that you cannot go on talking to me as you are. You will say something which you will regret!"

"Fiddlesticks! I want to marry you! Can't a fellow propose now?" he roared.

"Stop it! Stop it this minute!" cried Aurelia. The horse, taking all this shouting for a signal to move on, began to walk forward. Aurelia seized the reins from Harry's hands and pulled hard on them. The horse, unaccustomed to this kind of stop-go treatment, laid back its ears, snorted and bucked a little in the traces, and the gig rocked alarmingly.

"For heaven's sake, Aurelia, let go!" he snapped. "Here, give me those! What on earth do you think you're doing?"

"Getting down!" said Aurelia breathlessly, preparing to scramble unaided to the ground.

He seized her arm in a powerful grip and virtually hauled her back beside him. "No, you are not!"

"I am! Let me go!"

"You are not!" thundered Harry. "Sit still!"

Aurelia sat still.

"That's better," he said, releasing her arm. By this time a small and curious group had collected around them and was waiting in open anticipation for the next development in the drama being enacted before them. Harry turned on these spectators a look of such murderous intent that to a man they paled and fled. "And now, my dear," he said coolly to Aurelia, "who are these people who have made it their business to let you know that you are setting your cap at me?"

"Well, no one in particular . . . Harry, if I may not get down, then please take me home!"

"I absolutely refuse. I strongly suspect, Aurelia, that someone has been trying to interfere in a matter which, after all, is my concern as well as yours. Who is it, who, I take it, thinks we should not marry? For that is what this is all about, is it not?"

"We cannot marry," Aurelia said calmly and then stopped abruptly.

Everyone had been right—Gussie and Julia and Catherine. He did want to marry her, and only she, Aurelia, had been too obstinate to see what was happening and too stupid to realise that she, too, was falling in love. She wasn't afraid of Harry, nor did he make her angry: he attracted her. He had attracted her from the very beginning, and from the beginning she had fought it. She had refused to face the reality of her own emotions. But then, falling in love had been in no way part of her plans.

"I am sorry, Harry. I am truly sorry. I cannot marry you," she said in a very quiet little voice. "I think, if you knew all about me, you would not want to marry me."

"You are not going to tell me that you are not Aurelia Sinclair, but a desperate criminal fleeing from justice?" he asked with heavy irony.

"I am Aurelia Sinclair, and I'm not a criminal!" flared Aurelia, reverting to her normal belligerency toward him for a brief moment. The moment passed and her temper died down, flickered and expired, like the last flame of a fire which no longer has fuel to feed it. "I am not worthy of you, Harry. Oh, don't say anything. Please don't ask questions, and don't speak to me of this matter again!"

"I see!" he said after a lengthy silence. "Well, then, I shall consider myself refused, and we will not speak of it again. Forgive me for embarrassing you. Shall we drive on?"

"I would like to go home, Harry."

"Very well, I will take you home. I do hope," he hesitated, "I do hope you will not deprive me entirely of the pleasure of your company, Aurelia. Can we not be friends?"

"Yes," said Aurelia dully, "we can be friends."

As if friendship could ever be enough for either of them now!

CHAPTER
SEVEN

"So there it is," said Aurelia sadly to her reflection in the dressing mirror. "I shall have to go home. I shall have to tell the miserable Ribble that I haven't been able to raise the money and let him rub his hands and gloat. And his wretched employer will rub his fat hands and gloat too, and turn me out of my own home."

"You'm talking to yourself again, my dear!" came a voice from the sitting room. "Didn't I just tell 'ee about that? Seems to me Lunnon's fair turned your brain, child."

Aurelia stared silently at that other Aurelia in the mirror. That Aurelia seemed the same and yet was different. The dark curls, the heart-shaped face and the wide, violet eyes were the same, but the expression in the eyes was sober, the whole face had lost its sparkle, its animation and its air of youthful optimism.

Sarah bustled into the room and loomed over the reflection in the mirror. She, too, stared at it critically and shook her head in a worried way. "You'm going to make yourself ill with fretting, my lovely."

"I'm not sick," Aurelia said automatically.

"Look at you! Pining for a fancy gennelman . . ."

"Sarah!"

"Don't you 'Sarah' me! I'll speak out and you'll listen, my girl. You're pining for a fancy gennelman who—if he knew half o' the truth—wouldn't have asked for your hand anyway!"

"No, he wouldn't have," Aurelia agreed. She stirred herself and put down the ivory backed hairbrush in her hand. "Anyhow, Sarah, it's done me good. I was a fool to come here, on a fool's errand. Please don't say 'I told you so', because I know you did, and you were right. I am only sorry for the trouble to which I have put poor Lady Belphege in bringing me out. I hope the truth does not come out. It would be so very vexing and embarrassing for her."

"And his lordship?"

"Harry will get over me!" Aurelia returned briskly. "It's a good thing I was not able to accept him, for I'm sure he would change his mind sooner or later, anyway. I must enquire about sailings for Jamaica."

"Can't say I relish that journey again, Miss Aury," said Sarah with a groan.

Aurelia sighed as memories of a lurching, rolling, wooden ship, cramped berth, stale water and rancid pork came back to her. "One thing's certain!" she promised Sarah. "If I ever get back to Kingston in one piece, there I stay!"

Sarah made no reply to this but reached over her young mistress's shoulder to pick up a small white card from the dressing table. "Will you be going to this yere ball, then?"

"Yes, I must. Lady Belphege is sending her carriage for me. I can't cry off. I only hope . . . I only hope Lord Belphege won't be one of her party. I don't think I can face him so soon, not after refusing him only three days ago."

"You can't hide yourself for ever, my dear. 'Tis a question of going out there and facing up to them, or skulking in here like you was afraid."

"I'm not afraid. I haven't done anything wrong, I've just been very stupid," Aurelia said obstinately.

Sarah pulled aside the window curtains and peered

out morosely. "'Tis coming on to rain again, I'll swear. If you go out in that thin dress this evening, my pretty, you'll catch your death."

Aurelia dismissed this pessimistic forecast. "From door to door in a carriage? I shan't catch cold." She stood up and went to where the gold organdie dress hung, pristine and crisp. "I wish I hadn't bought this silly dress!" she said suddenly, with a touch of accustomed vigour. "For now it will be fairly wasted and I need all my money to get us back to Kingston! I will go tomorrow to the dressmaker and cancel those walking-dresses. Though if they are already cut out, I dare say she will want paying for them. Oh dear."

One fear was soon set at rest, however. Harry was not in Lady Belphege's party that evening.

"My son apologises," Lady Belphege said. "He would have escorted us this evening, but family business has called him away. However, Captain Foote has nobly stepped into the breach, eh, Captain?" She prodded Captain Foote playfully and painfully in the ribs with her cane.

He winced and gasped, "My pleasure, madam, I assure you!"

"I'm sure Harry would have liked to be here with us!" Julia said with an edge to her voice and a glare at Aurelia.

As usual, Julia was dressed disastrously in a truly hideous gown of coquelicot satin which clashed horribly with Aurelia's gold organdie. The clash of colours alone, Aurelia thought, must justify her keeping away from Julia all evening.

"I hope your back is better!" she said politely, determined that if there were to be any failure of courtesy, it would not be on her part.

Julia looked startled and managed to say, "Thank you. It is no worse," before struck by a thought which made her add sharply, "How should you know about that?"

"I trust we are not going to discuss your health, Julia!" said Lady Belphege unkindly, thus sparing Aurelia the need to answer.

Nobody could say that Captain Foote did not know his duty. Having settled Lady Belphege on a gilt sofa to gossip with an old friend, he first led Julia sedately round the floor, despite her protest that she had reached the age when no one expected her to dance, and then returned to offer his arm to Aurelia. As they circled the floor with all the other laughing, chattering couples, he smiled down at her.

"Well, Miss Sinclair! You are the belle of the ball!"

"Thank you, Captain Foote," Aurelia responded unenthusiastically.

He frowned slightly. "Forgive me, m'dear, for saying it, but you seem a little glum this evening."

"Not really, Gussie," she said, "I'm a little tired."

"It's a pity Harry's not been able to come," he observed, watching her closely. When she did not reply he added, "You know where he is, do you?"

"No," Aurelia said truthfully. "I've no idea."

"He's taken Kate and her two boys down to his country place, Eastfield Park. Kate's affairs are truly in a dreadful state. He's trying to talk some sense into her."

"He'll find it difficult!" Aurelia remarked sapiently.

"Oh, Harry can be very persuasive, and he needs to be in this case. He has been paying Kate's bills for a year or more. William is done up for money, you know. You've noticed William, have you?"

This explained much. Aurelia looked startled. "Here?"

"Yes. Don't look now, he's just behind us. I'll swing us round."

He turned her deftly so that she faced down the room. Sure enough, there was Fulton, dancing with an angular, yellow-haired female with diamond earrings. He looked as pale as ever, but more self-assured and animated.

Guessing her thoughts, Captain Foote whispered in her ear, "See how the poor fellow perks up when he's free of the harpy, Nancy, for an hour or two?"

"Gussie!" Aurelia exclaimed suddenly. "I want to talk to you."

"Now?" he asked.

"Now!" she said firmly.

"Then we had better go into the next room and procure a glass of punch. Come along." He took her arm and led her into the next room where a splendid cold buffet had been laid out on seemingly endless snowy tables. "Here we are, m'dear," he said, putting a glass into her fingers. "Let us sit down, over here." He handed her to a bench and sat beside her. The bench was too low for him and he was obliged to fold his long legs so that his knees stuck up in the air.

Aurelia smiled. "Poor Gussie. You don't look very comfortable."

"I am quite at my ease, I assure you. Speak on, fair lady, what troubles you?"

"You know," Aurelia said after some hesitation, "a lot of people seem to have taken it into their heads that I have matrimonial designs on Harry. I am afraid that Harry may have thought it too, and it misled him."

"Good lord!" he said with sudden insight. "He's proposed!"

"Yes. And I refused him," Aurelia said with commendable calm. "I want you to know that, Gussie."

"I see," he said thoughtfully. "Well, I am at fault, Miss Aurelia, because although I expected Harry to propose sooner or later, I certainly never thought you would really refuse him! I'm afraid I may have expressed words to that effect in some quarters. I apologise for any mischief done."

"After all I said to you, Gussie," she said reproachfully. "I told you I wouldn't marry Lord Belphege."

"Oh, I know you *said* that, but damme, I thought you'd see sense!" he blurted. After a while he added, "What will you do now, Aurelia?"

"Go back to Jamaica, surrender my property gracefully to. . . to the man who has a claim on it, rent a small villa, live meanly and grow an old maid," Aurelia declared simply.

He looked unhappy. "There must be a better alternative than that." He rubbed his kneecaps in an agitated manner and glowered at the floor for some minutes, then he said, "See here, Aurelia, I've a suggestion—and don't refuse it out of hand! I know I'm not Harry—and I haven't money enough to rescue your estate—but we could probably manage tolerably well on what I do have. It's a pity Boney is done for, for there's not much future in the Army in peace time, but we shouldn't starve. I'm suggesting you marry *me*, Aurelia. Don't go off in a fit and refuse without thinking it over, now!"

"You told me once before that it wouldn't do," she reminded him gently.

"Well, I thought then that you'd do a great deal better than me!" he said frankly. "But if all you're planning to do is to go back to Jamaica and moulder away doing embroidery and good works for the rest of your life, then I certainly put myself forward as an alternative to that."

"I couldn't marry you, not for those reasons, Gussie," Aurelia said. "It wouldn't be fair."

"I'd do my best by you, Aurelia," he said a little wistfully. "And I know I'd be very happy."

"No, Gussie, you wouldn't. There we should be, as poor as church mice together, me for ever lamenting the loss of my estate, and you wishing war would break out again so that you could get away. Why, six months of marriage to me and you would be plotting yourself to get Napoleon off St. Helena!"

"You can't know that," he objected. "We might do famously."

"*No*, Gussie!"

"Well, I've offered," he said resignedly. "Tell me if you change your mind. My offer stands." After a short silence during which he stared thoughtfully into his untasted glass of punch, and Aurelia fixed her gaze on a roast turkey surrounded by glazed apples on the buffet table, he asked, "You didn't tell him, I suppose, about your financial troubles?"

"No, Gussie, I didn't. I couldn't!"

"I still think you should."

"I can't, Gussie! It was awful. He apologised for suspecting me at first. How could I then tell him he had been right all along?"

"You do care for Harry, don't you?" was all he said.

"Yes, Gussie, I do," Aurelia agreed humbly.

"I thought you did," was his answer. "I always thought you did. You reacted too furiously at the mention of his name not to be interested at all."

"You are more perceptive than I am," she commented sadly. "I only realised it myself the other day, when I refused him."

"Well, well!" he said briskly, slapping his knees and tossing back his punch with a wry grimace, "never say die! Wellington always expected us to defend a position, even if it was hopeless. You mustn't give up now, m'dear. My word, this is foul punch!"

"Thank you for your encouragement, Gussie, but I fear my situation is beyond remedy. Now, please take me back to the ballroom," said Aurelia stonily.

She was glad to have this difficult exchange behind

her, but if she thought her difficulties were over for the evening, she was badly mistaken. A cotillion was called. Captain Foote gallantly led Julia on to the floor and Aurelia, to her scarcely disguised horror, saw William Fulton bearing down on her.

"Miss Sinclair, isn't it?" he said affably. The exercise of dancing had brought a little colour to his pale cheeks. "I know we have not met before in the best of circumstances, but as I know who you are, and you know who I am, perhaps you won't refuse to stand up with me for this set of dances?"

The music had already struck up and Aurelia, unable to formulate a protest in time, found herself led on to the floor. They got through the dancing tolerably well, but when the interval before the next set of dances came, Aurelia found to her dismay that her new partner was by no means disposed to leave her.

"I see you have come in my mother-in-law's party," he said.

It was very warm now in the ballroom and Aurelia was glad of the excuse to open up her fan and make a great play of cooling her heated face. "Yes, sir," was all she said.

"I have been to pay my respects to her," he said, "but they were not well received."

Aurelia would have liked to say that she was scarcely surprised, but contented herself with, "Indeed, sir?"

"You won't have heard any good of me from any of them!" he said defensively. "I'll wager they have told you all sorts of gossip and have painted me the greatest rake in Town, which I am very far from being, I assure you!"

"I hardly think . . ." Aurelia began.

"Don't pretend you know nothing of it," he interrupted, treating her to an impudent grin. "This is London, my dear Miss Sinclair, and no item of scandal is left without being embroidered, enhanced, re-cast and repeated!"

"I believe," Aurelia replied stiffly, "that if a person has nothing better to do than to listen to gossip, especially scandalous gossip, then he or she is in a sorry way!"

"That is a very noble sentiment," he told her, "but will gain no favour in this company. Besides, unless you are deaf, and I perceive you are not, you cannot have failed to hear of me from either Lady Belphege or one of her daughters—or her son." He grimaced.

"I cannot imagine, sir, why you should think people must spend their time talking of nothing but you and your affairs!" retorted Aurelia, who disliked his manner, which veered between the brash and the self-justifying. "I begin to suspect that you *hope* you are the subject of all conversation!"

"Ouf!" he exclaimed, opening his eyes very wide and pulling a comical face. "You have a sharp tongue, Miss Sinclair!"

"And you, sir, wish for sympathy without having shown that you deserve it!"

The erring husband treated her to a long, thoughtful stare. "Have you met my wife, Kate?" he asked suddenly.

Aurelia was obliged to admit that she had.

"Kate's a fine woman," he said, an absent look entering his eyes for a moment. Then he brought his sullen gaze back to her. "You think me an insolent dog, no doubt, Miss Sinclair, and I can't say I blame you for it."

"Mr Fulton," Aurelia said firmly, "I cannot see any good coming of our continuing this conversation. I assure you that Lady Belphege has never mentioned your name to me! I have met your wife. I am sorry for the troubles in your family, but have no wish to make them my concern!"

"Don't run away!" he begged as she made as if to turn away. "See here, they all say you are going to marry old Harry, and then we shall be related, shall we not?"

So that was the reason for his interest. Mr. Fulton, as his wife, feared a possible marriage for Harry which might put a stop to the generous financial aid they had received. They were thoroughly despicable, the pair of them, Aurelia thought furiously. She did not think Harry could be ignorant of their motives, and she could only applaud the family loyalty which led him to involve himself in their sordid domestic problems.

"I am going out on to the terrace," she snapped, "for air! Please do not attempt to follow me. Your company, sir, is not welcome!"

She did not care how rude he thought her. She pushed her way through the tall French windows on to the long, stone terrace. She discovered her mistake at once. Coming from the overheated ballroom, the air of the terrace struck icy cold. A fine drizzle was falling and the terrace was deserted, but because she feared Fulton might still be lying in wait for her, Aurelia resolved to stay outside for at least five or six minutes. She wrapped her inadequately thin shawl tightly around her and took refuge under a huge stone urn of geraniums and shivered. She had been wrong to come tonight. Harry himself was not here—but almost everyone connected with Harry was. The situation was intolerable, and it was about to be made worse. As she stood, pressed against the wall of the house, the sound of voices drifted out through the window.

"Such a pretty child, but are you sure he means to marry her?"

'Oh, but I have it on the very best authority!" replied a second voice.

"So strange one has not seen her before," observed the first.

"Oh, my dear, her entire fortune is in Jamaica! Miles of sugar estates, I'm told. One can see she is a little gauche and colonial in her ways, but the planters are all as rich as Solomon and live in a style one cannot imagine! Dear Lady Belphege must be so delighted . . ."

The voices died away and Aurelia was left to the cold and her misery.

"Aurelia!" called an anxious voice urgently through the gloom. "Is that you? What are you doing out here? It's raining! You'll be wet through."

"It's all right, Gussie," she responded, emerging from the shadows of the urn. She felt a surge of relief at the sight of his lanky figure framed in the French window. Music and laughter drifted out from behind him.

"What did Fulton want?" he asked brusquely. "I was dancing with Julia and couldn't dash across and rescue you. Come inside at once, dear girl, you're shaking like a leaf!" He put his arm around her shoulders comfortingly and guided her back into the lighted ballroom.

"I don't think I can dance anymore this evening, Gussie, I really don't," she told him. "I think I'll just go and sit with Lady Belphege, at least Fulton won't have the courage to seek me out there!"

"Unspeakable blackguard!" he growled. "Someone ought to call him out. But, miserable worm that he is, he probably can't even defend himself like a gentleman!"

"Oh, Gussie," she said, laughing in spite of herself because he sounded so ferocious, "I don't know whether I just despise the wretched man or feel sorry for him! He is another one who fears I may marry his brother-in-law."

"Oh, does he, indeed? Harry should leave that fellow to sink without trace. I know why he doesn't, though."

"Because of Kate?"

"Because of Kate's boys. Jolly little fellows, they deserve a better father. Harry likes the boys and anything he does for Kate is really done for his nephews."

He took her back to Lady Belphege, who took one look at Aurelia and rose majestically to her feet. "Give me your arm, Captain, if you please. It grows very late. Julia! Will you leave with us, Miss Sinclair, or shall I send my carriage back for you?"

"If you please, ma'am, I will come now, with you."

"Then let us be off. This has proved a most tiresome evening. I cannot abide such crowds. I have been pestered by that fool, Fulton, bowing and mumbling at me. The orchestra is very noisy and the punch is uncommon bad."

"I trust you enjoyed the supper at least, madam?" Captain Foote enquired meekly.

"Poor," said Lady Belphege. "One course, indeed! By the time we had all eaten, the platters were left empty! When I was a young gal, Captain, no lady would let an empty dish be seen upon her supper table. She made sure supplies were brought up from the kitchens! We shall go to my house directly, Captain, and there, in decent comfort, we shall partake of a proper supper and repair the ravages of this evening."

A footman was dispatched to tell Lady Belphege's coachman to bring the carriage round. After a little farewell conversation with their host and hostess, Lady Belphege declared that the carriage must surely be round by now. Without waiting for a message to that effect, the little party stepped out on to the portico to find, to its dismay and annoyance, that no carriage stood waiting. It really seemed to be one of those evenings.

"Come, Mama," urged Julia, shivering in the night air, "you cannot wait out here. You will suffer dreadfully tomorrow."

It was now raining heavily. The night was very dark and dismal and the torches which had been fixed in iron holders on the front of the house hissed and flickered unhappily and were reflected in the large puddles which had formed on the uneven cobbled forecourt. Beyond, in the now deserted street, a row of the new gas lamps shone dully, but only illuminated further the scene of desolation. Aurelia shuddered, both from the chill and from low spirits. Summer, indeed! She needed no urging to accompany Julia and Lady Belphege back into the house. Captain Foote followed them in.

By bad luck, Fulton stood at the foot of the stairs. His face shone with perspiration and his pale blue eyes bulged slightly as if his neckcloth were too tight. He looked yet more uncomfortable on seeing Lady Belphege, and came forward awkwardly to ask if anything was wrong. A faint aura of brandy hung about him.

"No!" said his mother-in-law tartly. "They are slow to put the horses to, that is all. You need not wait about with us, sir!"

Fulton took his dismissal meekly and retired into an adjoining room, passing Aurelia on the way. As he did so, he gave her a very searching look and brushed against her. Aurelia turned her head aside and twitched her arm away from his touch. She wondered why he had been hanging about in the vestibule, apparently to no purpose.

Their hostess now came hurrying up with profuse apologies.

"My dear Eleanor," said Lady Belphege graciously, "don't distress yourself and don't, I beg you, think you must keep us company out here. The carriage will be here directly, and your guests call for you."

Still apologising, their hostess retreated to the ballroom, promising to send immediately to the stables to see what had caused the delay. But at that moment the welcome rumble of wheels was heard. Gussie Foote popped out of the door and then in again with the promptitude of a jack-in-the-box and announced, "Here you are at last, Lady Belphege. Let me give you my arm. Mind the steps, now. Can you manage, ladies?" This last to Julia and Aurelia, who assured him through chattering teeth that they could manage very well.

Getting Lady Belphege into the carriage was not a rapid process. Julia and Aurelia stood at the top of the steps, sheltered from the rain, until it was their turn to make a dash for the carriage, and studiously avoided looking at one another. But after a moment Julia murmured something and hastened down the steps towards the carriage, apparently preferring to stand in the rain than to wait in the dry with her enemy. Aurelia sighed and, draping her shawl over her head, prepared to follow. Lady Belphege was safely in the carriage now, and Captain Foote was handing in Julia.

"Miss Sinclair!" hissed a voice.

Aurelia jumped and looked round, startled, peering into the gloom. A dim figure emerged from the shadows behind a pillar. In the uncertain light of the torches she recognised William Fulton again.

"I fear I displeased you earlier, Miss Sinclair," he said hastily in a hoarse whisper, with a nervous glance towards the waiting carriage and the impatient form of a damp Captain Foote signalling to Aurelia to hurry.

"Whatever are you doing out here?" demanded Aurelia. 'Are you following me about, sir?"

"Well, yes, I . . ." he began, but was not allowed to finish.

"Off you go, Billy!" ordered Gussie peremptorily, as he bounded up the steps and seized hold of Aurelia's arm. "What the devil do you think you're about, eh? Keeping the lady hanging about in the rain at this time of night!"

Fulton gave him a furious glare but dared not reply in view of the warlike gleam in the captain's eye. He shrugged and turned to stride back into the house again, without a further word.

"I don't trust that fellow!" muttered Gussie to Aurelia as he handed her up into the carriage. "He's a wrong 'un. Watch out for him, Aurelia."

CHAPTER
EIGHT

It was not until the early hours of the morning that Aurelia finally got to bed. Even so, she did not fall asleep immediately. She lay awake for almost an hour, thinking of Harry, of Gussie, of Fulton and his wife, of Julia and Antony Helliwell. She tossed uneasily on her pillows, listening to the steady beating of the rain on the windowpanes and the gentle snoring from Sarah, who slept on a truckle bed on the further side of the room.

She wondered if it was raining at Eastfield Park, too, and whether Harry lay awake, as she did, listening to the rain and even, perhaps, thinking of her. If he was, then what kind of thoughts were they? Affectionate? Hardly, after being refused out of hand by her with no explanation. Resentful, then? But Harry was too generous a spirit to bear a grudge against her on the sole grounds of wounded vanity.

Or what about Gussie and his quixotic offer of marriage? Aurelia smiled faintly in the darkness. Poor Gussie, the soul of honour, feeling that by his unthinking gossip he had contributed to the whole wretched misunderstanding, and wanting desperately to make amends. Or bluff, dull, honest, unimaginative Antony Helliwell, who was in a position to ruin her, but by some miracle, did not seem to know it. Helliwell, Helliwell, Helliwell . . .

Aurelia drifted into sleep. She had a confused dream in which she was back in Jamaica and it was very hot, so hot that she could hardly breathe. The agent, Ribble in his black waistcoat, swam up out of the haze carrying a large water jug and a glass. He offered this last to her, but when she put out a hand to take it, it eluded her, and Ribble himself somehow turned into Fulton, with his pale face and prominent stare.

She awoke shortly before eleven with a dull, muzzy feeling and a dry mouth. She struggled into a sitting position. The truckle bed had been pushed away and she was alone. She called for Sarah, who bustled in and pulled the curtains. Sunlight streamed in and the raindrops from the previous night which had not yet dried on the window threw a speckled effect on to everything in the room, so that it was like looking at objects through a veil. In the corner stood a large basket of roses.

Aurelia blinked. "Sarah? What's that? Where did it come from?" Her voice sounded hoarse and unnatural and she tried to clear her throat.

"They roses?" said Sarah, glancing disparagingly at the fine blooms. "A boy brought 'un. An hour since, 'twas, while you was still sleeping."

"This morning? But from whom? There must be some mistake."

Sarah's answer to this was to pluck a small white card from the midst of the bouquet. She brought this back to Aurelia and handed it over in disapproving silence.

"Miss Sinclair," read Aurelia aloud. "W.F. sends apologies and sincerely begs forgiveness for importuning Miss S. He trusts she will forgive him and believe his protestations of heartfelt and respectful devotion."

"If'n that don't beat all!" said Sarah, half in disgust and half in unwilling admiration. "That's the queerest bit o' writing I ever heard. Poor fellow sounds as though he were only elevenpence to the shilling."

"W.F.," repeated Aurelia. "William Fulton! You're

right, Sarah, his brain isn't working as it should. Really, the stupid man! Did he think I'd complain to Lord Belphege about him?"

"Well, who is this William Fulton, then?" demanded Sarah impatiently.

"He is married to one of Lord Belphege's sisters. No doubt he refers to his brother-in-law as 'Lord B.'! Those roses are a little tactful insurance, I fancy. As if my good will may be bought with flowers! Throw them out, Sarah," Aurelia ordered crossly, tossing the card down on the coverlet and falling back on the pillows.

Sarah peered down at her suspiciously, consternation on her kindly features. "You don't look at all well, my dear. You feeling sick?"

"No, no! Only annoyed by that ridiculous man. Oh, do take those wretched flowers out!"

"Whatever you say, Miss Aury," said Sarah, gathering up the roses in a huge armful and transporting them to the door. There she paused and looked back at the bed. "You try and get a little more sleep, my lovely, and I'll come back soon with some tea and toast. You've taken cold, that's what."

As the day progressed Aurelia's symptoms multiplied to include an insistent pain at the bridge of her nose. It spread quickly upwards to become a headache and downwards to her throat, which became sore.

Sarah fussed about the shivering figure, scolding and consoling in the same breath. "'Tis like I said! Going out in they thin dresses with it raining cats and dogs! Lie still, my lovely, and let Sarah bathe your forehead. Bless us, the child's going into a fever. Will you hold still?"

"It's nothing, Sarah!" protested Aurelia in a hoarse croak, but Sarah was not to be deceived and Aurelia was swiftly cocooned in a blanket and ordered to "sweat it out".

She dozed fitfully all day. Shortly before two a messenger brought a note from Lord Belphege, saying that he had just arrived back in Town, and would be honoured if she would allow him to call. Aurelia roused herself sufficiently, despite a raging temperature and a feeling of general muzziness, to scrawl an apologetic reply telling him that it was quite impossible, as she had taken a chill. "The English weather is being revenged on me for all I have said about it!" she wrote as a postscript.

It was that postscript, together with the unevenness of the handwriting, which persuaded him, he afterwards said, that she really was ill and not simply avoiding him. He called in person the next day to enquire after her and was received downstairs by Sarah. Mrs. Fraddon afterwards maintained she could not remember exactly what she had told him, but whatever it was, it proved sufficiently alarming to occasion another note begging Aurelia to allow him to send his mother's doctor to see her.

Aurelia scribbled a terse "Thank you—no! It's only a cold."

She was surprised to be awoken later that evening by a considerable racket coming from the staircase. Dragged from restless slumber, her mind would not focus properly. It sounded as though several people were coming upstairs and a voice, domineering and vaguely familiar, overrode all the other noise and was coming nearer. It was accompanied by the regular thud of a stick on wood. The door burst open and Lady Belphege, leaning heavily on her ebony cane, made an impressive entrance, followed by a dry, professional-looking man in black knee-breeches and coat over a russet waistcoat, and a plainly dressed female of indeterminate years and depressed aspect who was presumably a personal maid, with Sarah bringing up the rear of the procession.

Lady Belphege drew to a halt by the bed and the rest

of the company piled up behind her in some confusion. They sorted themselves out with muttered apologies to each other, the plain female casting a disparaging look at her surroundings and the black-clad gentleman adjusting his coat and clearing his throat as if to embark on some speech. Lady Belphege tapped the ferrule of her cane sharply on the floor to bring them all to order and inclining slightly over the bed, stared hard down at Aurelia.

"Wretched!" she pronounced.

Shock had awakened Aurelia's senses and she struggled to a sitting position and attempted to straighten her lace cap, unhappily conscious of her creased nightgown, rumpled bedclothes and perspiration-stained pillows. Sarah elbowed her way past the plain female and straightened the top sheet with a "tut-tut" and a meaning look at her mistress. But Aurelia might as well have been an object of medical interest displayed to a class of students, for Lady Belphege, very much in the manner of a lecturing surgeon, signalled imperiously to the dry man and ordered, "Take a good look, Dr. Phillips, and give me your opinion."

They made way for him and the black-clad man approached the bed, bowed, and said gravely, "Good evening, ma'am."

"Good evening!" whispered Aurelia.

Lady Belphege hissed in annoyance at time wasted by useless courtesies and tapped sharply on the floor with the ferrule of her cane, but the doctor ignored her and, bending forward, politely requested Aurelia to put out her tongue. Aurelia did so and the assembled company surveyed it.

"Ah, yes," commented the doctor, affably. "If I might have your wrist?"

Aurelia presented him with her wrist and he took her pulse, consulting a large gold watch at the same time.

"Ah, yes," he said again in a kindly manner. He then felt the patient's forehead and enquired whether she was suffering from any pains, or, as he put it, other inconveniences.

"I can't seem to keep warm, though I'm wet through with perspiration," she admitted.

"Sweating it out," said Sarah mysteriously.

The doctor nodded sagely and straightened up. "A severe chill, ma'am!" he observed to Lady Belphege. "Warm room, beef tea and a light diet. Beware of draughts!" he added, glancing round the room censoriously. He returned his watch to a pocket in the russet waistcoat, adjusted his coat, folded his hands and stood perfectly still.

"My dear Miss Sinclair!" declared Lady Belphege, addressing Aurelia directly for the first time. "You hear Dr. Phillips? You may believe him. I consult him myself. It is out of the question, of course, that you remain here. You must receive proper attention!"

Sarah bridled and showed signs of umbrage, but was ignored.

"You shall come and stay with me," Lady Belphege went on. "Your maid shall put your things together and I shall send the carriage back for you in one hour. Please be ready and wrap up warmly. See to it that your mistress is properly clad!" she added severely to Sarah.

"Yes, ma'am!" said Sarah, bobbing a cumbersome curtsy as she recognised a superior authority. "I'm allus telling her she don't wear enough clothes."

And so, as it seemed in no time at all, Aurelia found herself comfortably tucked up in bed in a large and elegantly furnished room with a fire burning brightly in the grate, reflecting its pink-red glow off the damask hangings and stucco ceiling. She leaned back on the lace-trimmed pillows and smoothed the carefully folded top sheet with one hand. She felt as though she had been given a free wish by a good fairy, and as a result had been transported in the twinkling of an eye from economical and cheerless lodgings to all the luxury of wealth. She sighed. The good fairy—in the unlikely guise of Lady Belphege—had been too kind. It would be impossible to carry out her plans from beneath this roof. Her independence had been abruptly curtailed, and as soon as she was better she would need to find an excuse for moving out again. She had a feeling this might prove difficult.

In fact, curiously enough, her one ally in engineering her removal from this house might well prove to be her avowed enemy, Julia. Aurelia glanced at the long case clock in the corner. During her arrival and installation in the bedroom she had noticed nothing of Julia. But she assumed that a visit from that lady would not be long in coming. In the meantime she had nothing to do but relax in comfort, though her head still ached and her throat was still sore. She took a drink of the barley water thoughtfully set on a table by the bed and settled herself on the pillows. Well, it was no use fretting about the future when she was in no condition to think clearly. But she must try and have her wits about her when Julia came in.

The door opened, but it was Sarah who entered, looking almost cheerful. She stationed herself at the foot of the bed, arms folded, and beamed happily at the invalid. "'Tis a beautiful house, Miss Aury! You should see they kitchens! I never seen the like. All the pots and pans shining like stars, and a furriner doing the cooking what can't speak proper English nohow, poor fellow. This is living, this is."

"Yes, Sarah," agreed Aurelia with a wry smile. A puzzled frown crossed her brow. "Sarah, what did you tell Lord Belphege?"

Sarah looked vague. "I don't rightly remember that,

my dear. I just told 'un you was sick. My, he took on. The poor man went pale, I'll swear, and him such a fine, healthy, handsome figure o' a man." Her look became thoughtful. "Miss Aury, 'tis a pity you turned down his offer, for you won't get no better one, not in a month of Sundays. And see here, I was thinking . . ."

"Yes, Sarah?"

"Well, what if you didn't tell 'un about your pa's debts till after the wedding? 'Twould be too late for him to back off, wouldn't it? You'd be married, and that's final! After all, there's lots of folks get married and then find out things about each other they didn't know before."

"*No*, Sarah!" Aurelia insisted strongly, despite her aches and pains.

"Well, there's no harm in suggesting it," Sarah said obstinately. "And 'twouldn't do no harm for you to think it over, an' all, my dear."

It was quite late, only a little before the entire household would be preparing for bed, that a sharp knock on the bedroom door announced Julia's arrival. She crossed the room quickly to stand by the bed and look down at Aurelia. Her round face was quite expressionless as she said coldly, "My mother sends to ask if you are quite comfortable, Miss Sinclair, and whether you need anything."

"I am very comfortable, thank you, and I'm sure I don't lack a thing. Your mother is very kind."

Julia's face twitched and she turned aside and walked jerkily towards the fire. "Dr. Phillips says you have a severe chill," she said, staring into the crackling flames. "From what Harry told us we all thought you must be dying!"

"Harry—I mean, Lord Belphege—didn't see me. Sarah probably exaggerated my woes."

The slip of the tongue over the use of her brother's

Christian name was not unnoticed by Julia, and Aurelia cursed her own clumsiness.

"You are no doubt congratulating yourself on having been very clever," Julia said from the fireplace. The red light flickered on her face, lending colour to her pale cheeks. "And I congratulate you too, Miss Sinclair. You are quite the centre of attention. My brother is worried out of his wits, and my mother is determined to throw herself entirely into the task of caring for you. Cook has been instructed to make calf's foot jelly, and all the maids ordered to tiptoe past the door for fear of disturbing you. At this very moment, straw is being put down outside the house to muffle the noise of passing carriages!"

Aurelia pushed herself upright with a jerk. "Julia! Even you cannot think I would go and catch cold intentionally!"

"Oh, don't bother!" said Julia abruptly. "Whether you intended all this or not is neither here nor there. The result is all that matters, and you can hardly fail to be satisfied with that!" She stared across the room to the girl in the bed, hostility marked on her homely features. "I hope you sleep well, Miss Sinclair," she said with studied politeness.

Meanwhile, in Lady Belphege's drawing-room, Harry and his mother were also discussing Aurelia's health.

"You did quite right to come to me, Harry," said his mother with approval. "The child would have sickened into a putrid fever in those dreadful rooms. So damp! She was receiving no proper nursing. I don't doubt for a minute that the woman, Fraddon, is absolutely devoted, but I'm sure that if permitted, she would dose the child with country remedies and make matters worse."

Harry nodded. "That's what I feared. I'm very grateful to you, Mama, for bringing Aurelia here."

She made a little "tsk, tsk!" noise and began to smooth

out the fringe on her shawl meticulously. "You do realise, Harry, that now I have brought the gal here, people will be expecting an engagement to be announced?"

"They will all be disappointed. Aurelia has already refused me."

"Quite rightly! No well-bred gal accepts a man the first time he proposes, or at least, she didn't in my day. Not unless she was afraid he mightn't offer again!"

"Unfortunately, Mama," said her son with a dry smile, "I don't think that in Aurelia's case it was just some fashionable nonsense about how a young lady should behave, or even plain coquetry, which made her refuse. I think she simply does not wish to marry me. No doubt she has her reasons."

"Then she would be a fool, and I don't believe she is that!" His mother raised her eyebrows archly. "At least while she is in this house, I expect we shall all see a little more of you, Harry!"

He had the grace to look a little abashed at this thrust, but Lady Belphege did not pursue her advantage and changed the subject briskly. "Since you are here, Harry, and we are alone, I think we should discuss the matter of your recent visit to Eastfield."

"You want to discuss Catherine, is that it? I have left her and the boys safely settled at Eastfield. I expect the boys are raising a riot by now."

"What the boys may do does not worry me. I am concerned with Catherine and her nonsensical way of floating through life on a cloud of sensibility. I hear you have been paying her bills."

"Now, where did you hear that?" he asked, narrowing his eyes thoughtfully.

"One may hear it anywhere in London! It is common knowledge. I see that it displeases you. I take it, then, that the report is true."

"Partly true. I have not been paying all Kate's bills,

only one or two pressing ones. I can't stand by and let her be dunned by tradesmen."

"Have you spoken to William?" demanded his mother.

"I did, some time ago. Unfortunately his, ah, commitments don't permit him to increase the allowance he makes his wife."

"By commitments you mean his doxy! I saw him with her only the other day. The hussy was dressed like a duchess, though in very poor taste, and the wretched William looked like a man on the way to the gallows. I fancy he is scarcely forty, and quite looks sixty! Indeed, one lady nearby asked, 'Who is that old man with the pretty jade?' He is making a fool of himself, of Kate and of us, all over London. It is past bearing! The fellow is obviously out of his senses and must be committed to Bedlam!"

"Good lord!" exclaimed Harry, startled. "I don't think we can do that, madam!"

"Why ever not? He is headed for Newgate, anyway."

"Prison and a lunatic asylum are not quite the same thing, Mama. William is a fool, but a sane fool. I don't say he is entirely unaware of his situation. In his heart he would probably like to put it right. But I must admit he is such a spineless noodle that I have very little hope for him! Talking to him is like dealing with a drunken man whom you wish to persuade to walk in a straight line. He knows what is required of him, but cannot do it. That is William."

"It is not a reason for you to ruin yourself trying to meet Kate's expenses as well as your own!" observed his mother.

"Then who is to do it?" he asked bluntly.

"Kate must retrench! She must take a smaller house, dismiss half her servants, cease to keep a carriage and find a less expensive dressmaker. There, those things for a start! I have written to her in very strong terms. She will receive my letter at Eastfield. I have told her she will not have a penny from me unless she does as I advise. Moreover, I have told her that I insist upon a legal separation. You must instruct lawyers, Harry, to draw up a deed of separation between William and Kate, and see that they sign it. And see that is as advantageous to Kate as possible."

"No!" he said sharply.

His mother raised her eyebrows and looked at him expectantly.

"I must crave your pardon, madam," he said, "for speaking so firmly, but in all honesty I do not believe that you have thought the matter out."

"Do you not, indeed?" remarked his mother drily.

Harry came to sit by her and leaned forward earnestly. "I know how you feel about the matter, madam. Good heavens, we could all of us cheerfully murder William now, but if you will just consider how the situation will stand in a few years' time, then I'm sure you'll see that things must be patched up between them. Take William—we none of us have a high opinion of him, but by the time his money has been entirely squandered and his reputation as a rake has shut all doors to him, he will be left with nothing to do but drink his days away in the lowest company. Is that the rôle you envisage for the father of your grandchildren? If we are not under a direct obligation to protect William from himself, then we are obliged to try and protect the children from the scandal occasioned by William's follies." He paused for breath.

"Go on!" said Lady Belphege expressionlessly.

"Nor can Kate go on as she has been doing," he continued. "She's a handsome woman with many friends, but both you and I know that once she is completely penniless and her looks begin to fade, those friends will fade too! Kate will be just another deserted wife with two boys on her hands and a dissolute rake of a husband. So, William must be persuaded, forced, bribed—the means don't matter—to see sense. He must send away the girl, Nancy. She's a pert miss and I'm sure won't lack protection for long. Naturally it will cost money, but we can find it. He must be seen publicly with his wife. He must stop acting like a fool. Kate must see sense too and agree to have him back. Good Lord, she's always calling him 'poor, dear William'! It's not as though they hate one another. William always speaks of Kate with respect, and Kate only cast William aside because his presence interfered with all her many social interests. Well, she must see it is time to give up the parties and devote a little time to her husband. They are an irritating and stupid pair, and it is up to us to knock their heads together!" concluded Harry robustly.

Lady Belphege approved, at least, of the idea of knocking Mr. Fulton's head against something. "You are right, Harry, of course," she added. "I leave it to you. I shall be *civil*," she finished dramatically, "to William!"

"And you will leave me to handle the affair?"

"With pleasure. I have not the patience for it. Really, Catherine irritates me almost more than Julia does, and goodness knows, Julia would try the patience of a saint!"

"Julia is of great use to you, Mama, I fancy!" he said sharply.

"Oh, she is useful in her bookish, bluestocking way! But she has no spirit, none at all."

For a moment he looked angry, but then controlled himself and said, "I will see what may be done to help Kate. Goodnight, Mama."

She gave him her hand to kiss. "Goodnight, Harry. Don't *you* make a fool of yourself. Marry little Aurelia. She will keep you on your toes!"

CHAPTER
NINE

AURELIA made a rapid return to health under her kind friend's roof but, as she had feared, Lady Belphege seemed in no way disposed to let her go once she had recovered. In fact, on the very first day she emerged from her bedroom she found that other plans had already been made.

"Nonsense, child! Why ever do you want to leave here and take rooms again?" Lady Belphege asked briskly when Aurelia ventured to introduce the topic of her departure. It was impossible to describe the tone of voice in which she said 'rooms'. "I am very pleased to have you here. Besides, although I like a young woman to show independence of mind myself, there are others who are mean-spirited enough to find it odd in you to want to live alone, Aurelia. You are too young. It is a little *outré*. One must always observe the conventions, my dear. At least," she added with worldly confidence, "until you are married. After that you will find people lose interest in you quickly enough. As a matter of fact, my dear, I have—together with my son—made other arrangements and we hope you will not object to them."

"What are they?" asked Aurelia, in some alarm.

"Don't look so frightened, my dear!" said her ladyship kindly. "You see, I am going down to Eastfield next week. We shall be a family party. Julia comes, naturally. Catherine and her two boys are already there, as will be Harry, who travels down tomorrow. I feel the air of the country will do you good and, as the season in Town is practically over in any case, I consider it the very best thing that you should come too. You cannot fail to like Eastfield. It is a very pretty place."

"We should not be too many?" faltered Aurelia, knowing full well that Lady Belphege had made up her mind and nothing would persuade her to change it or to take 'no' for an answer.

"Oh, there is plenty of room at Eastfield!" replied Lady Belphege serenely.

Lord Belphege departed for his country place the following day and a few days later Lady Belphege, Aurelia, Julia and Addams the maid, squeezed uncomfortably into an antiquated springless travelling coach, set off at a sedate pace into Hampshire. Julia's maid, Sarah and a manservant followed behind with a mountain of luggage in an even more elderly conveyance. Lady Belphege did not believe in spending money unnecessarily.

It could not be the most pleasant of journeys. Julia was scrupulously polite but monosyllabic. Lady Belphege sat bolt upright, not relaxing to lean back against the squabs once during the entire journey, and obviously expected the other two ladies to maintain the same rigid attitude. The coach lurched and rocked. Conversation was at a minimum, and Addams had a cold and sniffed loudly at intervals.

"Blow your nose, woman!" Lady Belphege ordered her crossly after the tenth bout of prolonged sniffing. Addams trumpeted loudly into an enormous white handkerchief.

Yet, as they travelled away from London's clamour, Aurelia's spirits rose. The countryside was beginning to turn to the red of autumn. Here and there, fields which had not yet been harvested rippled golden under the sun. The downland rolled away majestically to either side and as they passed the isolated thatched cottages or rumbled through small hamlets, the local people in smocks and gaiters, cotton bonnets and voluminous aprons, came to the low doors of their dwellings to see the gentry go by, and there was much pulling of forelocks and bobbing of clumsy curtsys whilst the rosy cheeked children jumped up and down in the dust for sheer excitement. This was another England, far from the noise and smoke and confusion of London. Aurelia almost felt she was in another land.

Their progress was slow and their journey punctuated by frequent calls at wayside inns. As they clattered, creaking and swaying ominously into the yard, a cry would go up: "The Quality is here!" They would descend, surrounded by startled 'regulars', obsequious landlord and landlady and a horde of curious and bustling domestics. Lady Belphege's routine at these stopping places never varied. She would first commandeer the room often named, with more optimism than accuracy, 'the Sun' and in this dank and cheerless parlour the party would install itself. A frightened servant would scuttle in to light the fire which, having inevitably been laid some days previously, would belch forth smoke and fumes to engulf the occupants of the room. Undaunted, Lady Belphege would insist on tea being brewed in her presence so that she might supervise the operation. She also brought her own tealeaves in a silver caddy which was kept locked and the key secreted somewhere about Lady Belphege's person. Boiling water would be called for, partly for the tea and partly for the 'portable soup' which Addams, her ladyship's melancholy handmaiden, would produce wrapped in a napkin. This was a bricklike substance prepared by Lady Belphege's cook before the travellers' departure from London. When mixed with boiling water it disintegrated and produced a curious-tasting bouillon which Lady Belphege declared "most healthy" and infinitely preferable to the product of the inn's kitchens.

It occurred to Aurelia that Lady Belphege, whilst making ample use of the facilities offered by the inn, actually spent very little money there. This did not seem to matter to the landlord, who always seemed content just to have such an illustrious party under his roof. Despite her qualms about being at Eastfield Park House, Aurelia, after a couple of experiences with the smoky parlours and the 'portable soup', began to wish that they might arrive there as soon as possible.

At last they turned through a tall arched stone gateway and rolled past a lodge cottage and began to jingle up the neatly raked gravel drive between twin lines of lime trees towards Eastfield Park itself.

"Here we are!" said Lady Belphege, relief sounding even in her voice.

Aurelia put her head out of the window and exclaimed with delight. Eastfield Park was not a particularly large country house, but it was perfectly proportioned and designed in the Palladian style. Around it stretched beautifully kept gardens and beyond them woodland.

"Is it not pretty?" asked Lady Belphege with satisfaction. "My late husband was largely responsible for the finished appearance of the house though he, naturally, did not begin it. The idea to rebuild in the present style was that of *his* father. The core of the house dates from Charles II, but little of that remains now. Ah, there is Harry, come to greet us!"

Sure enough, there was Harry running down the steps between the ornamental urns to greet them and assist his mother to descend to *terra firma*. "You are safely here, then, Mama!" He kissed her cheek and turned to Julia, who also received a kiss. For a moment Aurelia was dreadfully afraid he was going to kiss her too, but he only bowed and said, "It is a great pleasure to welcome you to

Eastfield, Miss Sinclair!"

They trooped up the steps, past smiling, bobbing housekeeper and assorted domestics, and into the hall. There was an explosion and two small boys, as alike as peas in a pod and obviously twins, tumbled headlong down the splendid staircase and rushed up to the party with arms waving and voices vying to be heard.

"Here is Grandmama! Grandmama, Uncle Harry has given us a pony!"

"And Richard tried to make him jump over a log and he wouldn't go!" cried one of them.

"And I fell off and landed on my head!" cried the other.

"And he's got a bruise!" shrieked the first. "Show Grandmama and Aunt Julia, Richard!"

Richard pushed up his tousled mop of fair hair to reveal a purple circle which he displayed with pride.

"Dear me!" said Lady Belphege, bending to inspect this honourable wound. "That is indeed a splendid bruise. I trust that your Uncle Harry is not encouraging you to break your necks?"

"We put a grass snake in Uncle Harry's bed!" said Richard smugly.

"And he put his feet on it because he didn't know it was there!" added his twin, whose name, Aurelia found, was Robert.

"And," said Richard in awestruck tones, "Uncle Harry swore!"

"Uncle Harry can swear better than Father!" Robert informed them. "And he chased us right through the house in his nightshirt!"

"Ah yes," said Uncle Harry, hastily interrupting these revealing confidences. "That is enough of that, I fancy! Let us go into the library and take some refreshment. I dare say you are parched."

Lady Belphege patted Robert on the head and enquired, "And where is your mama, my dear?"

"She's waiting in there!" Robert informed them, pointing at the nearest door. "Because she said she didn't intend to squash into the hall with a crowd of people!"

"Robert!" said his uncle. "I do feel that you and your brother should remove yourselves for the moment and allow Grandmama to rest. Cut along, now!"

They progressed to the long, narrow library where they did indeed find Catherine, fetchingly attired in white muslin sprigged with rosebuds and a pink sash, elegantly draped on a red velvet chaise-longue. She allowed them all time to admire the composition she formed before rising to her feet and coming to greet her mother and sister.

"How wise of you to wait in here, Catherine!" said her mother tartly. "That is a pretty gown and apparently new. I trust you have not been running up bills again?"

Catherine looked embarrassed, as well she might, at having this forthright remark addressed to her before an outsider and, glancing at Aurelia, she said just a little crossly, "No, Mama, I have not. Indeed, I spend nothing these days!"

Lady Belphege accepted a glass of wine and did not deign to reply. She could not have done so, in any case, for the doors at the far end of the library burst open and what appeared to be a small pack of assorted dogs raced into the library barking and wagging their tails, and proceeded to jump up on the furniture and on to the new arrivals indiscriminately.

"Robert! Richard!" roared Harry in stentorian tones, "Come and fetch these blessed animals out of here! I told you to keep 'em out! Get down, Smuts, bad dog! And you, too, Spot! Get down at once, I say, sir!"

"He has put his paws on me!" shrieked Catherine as a

King Charles spaniel took a flying leap and landed on the sprigged muslin.

It was Aurelia who, with great presence of mind, lifted the little dog off and sat him down on her own lap and held him firmly.

"He sheds hairs like a devil!" observed his master, red in the face from the exertion of trying to round up and eject his assorted pets. His nephews appeared with angelic faces and obligingly removed the animals they had so obviously loosed.

"Are the boys behaving well?" enquired their grandmother in a voice devoid of any irony.

"Very well!" said their mother promptly. "My boys always behave as they should!"

"Little Turks!" said their Uncle Harry breathlessly, as he slammed the doors. "I told 'em to keep those dratted dogs out! They put a dead mouse in the soup tureen yesterday!"

"I cannot believe that it was either Richard or Robert!" Catherine said adamantly. "There are mice in the kitchen and the servants only wished to avoid blame."

"And salt in the teapot," continued Harry, ignoring this defence, "and made a black rim with coal dust in the rector's hat, and I have to pay for the cleaning of the poor man's wig."

Catherine looked affronted.

"Boys will be boys," said their grandmother graciously. "But I trust they will not attempt to play their tricks on me! You must watch out, Miss Sinclair. Look into your bed before you get into it and tap your shoes before you put them on, for there may be a beetle or some such dead insect hidden in them."

In fact, Aurelia was to find that once the twins had discovered that Miss Sinclair did not scream at the sight of spiders and was not frightened of ghosts but only curious to see one, they made no attempt to plague her and reserved their undoubted talents for making apple-pie beds and setting booby traps for their Aunt Julia, who never failed to shriek in a gratifying manner.

When Aurelia went upstairs to change her gown she found that she had been given a very pretty room with a southerly aspect over the gardens. She leaned out of the windows and looked out over the woods and fields before her. She wondered how much of this land belonged to Harry. No doubt quite a goodly part of it. There was a smell of woodsmoke in the air and below her, on the terrace, Richard and Robert were engrossed in building some strange machine with sticks and string.

"What is it?" she called down.

They looked up, their identical snub-nosed, freckled faces solemn. "A kite," said Richard.

"But it doesn't fly," said his twin.

"I'll show you how to do it tomorrow," Aurelia promised. "I do know how to make kites." She pulled in her head and turned to where Sarah was unpacking her boxes and laying out her gowns. Sarah was humming a little melody under her breath.

Aurelia smiled. "Well, I see you are content at any rate, Sarah."

"That I am," Sarah agreed comfortably. "I never could take to towns. All those bricks and chimneys spitting smoke. I was born a country girl, and a countrywoman I've stayed." She cocked an eye at Aurelia. "'Tis pretty here, a'n't it, Miss Aury?"

"Yes, Sarah, it's very pretty."

"'Twould be a handsome thing," observed Sarah ruminatively, "to be mistress of a fine house like this'n, wi' the park an' all. Farms, too."

"I dare say it would be, Sarah," said Aurelia calmly. "But I hope you will not be imagining that *I* shall ever be the mistress of Eastfield, for you know as well as I do, that it isn't possible and never can be."

"Love's a powerful thing," was Sarah's rather enigmatic reply.

Aurelia turned away back towards the window without answering.

"Your mama and your pa," said Sarah artfully, "would have been happy enough to see you mistress of a house like this 'un."

"After December I shall not even be mistress of my own Kingston house," Aurelia said sharply. "Perhaps you had better remember that, Sarah!"

"Dang that Kingston house!" muttered Sarah resentfully. She hung up the organdie gown and turned to face Aurelia. "An' what use is that there house, or any house, with no man in it? You tell me that, missie! An' I'll tell you another thing. Even this great house a'n't no comfort to his lordship, I'll swear, with no wife nor childer of his own in it!"

The two little Fultons were not slow to corner the new visitor early the next day with a demand that she honour her promise to show them how to make a kite. Aurelia obliged and an hour later, by which time both little boys were thoroughly bedáubed with paste and had scraps of cloth and paper stuck to their faces, hands and clothing, the three of them proceeded out on to the terrace to try the new kite. It was just the right kind of day, warm but with a firm breeze. With some difficulty the kite was persuaded into the air and hung uncertainly above them for some moments before descending abruptly out of sight over the edge of the terrace.

"Well, it's better than ours have ever done!" said Robert kindly, as his twin raced away to recover it. Evidently he felt that his new friend might be embarrassed by the accident. "Ours wouldn't even fly at all, and we ran round the garden with them all day."

Richard returned puffing with the kite in his hands. Minor repairs were needed and as these were being effected he suddenly said, "Father comes tomorrow."

Aurelia was taken aback. "Your father—Mr Fulton—is coming here?"

It was not the most tactful response, but neither twin noticed the implication, or the situation between their parents was considered so commmonplace to them that they did not expect outsiders to react any differently to the way Aurelia had done.

"Uncle Harry said, Papa will be here tomorrow," maintained Richard. Apparently if Uncle Harry said so, it must be right. "Uncle Harry said he had the devil of a job persuading him, but that he was coming."

"Uncle Harry did not say that to you, I think!" observed Aurelia reprovingly.

"No," Richard agreed calmly, "he said it to Aunt Julia. But I was outside the window with my kite—the one which wouldn't go up— and I heard them. Aunt Julia said Papa wouldn't come, even if he'd promised it. But Uncle Harry said he'd made sure of it."

Aurelia could not help but wonder why Harry had insisted on his brother-in-law coming, but Richard had the anwer to that, too.

"There is to be a," he paused and then brought out the latest word in his vocabulary proudly, "a *reconciliation*. That means Papa and Mama are going to make it up and go to parties together, instead of going separately to different ones."

"I see," said Aurelia faintly. "Richard, my dear, I do not feel that you should discuss the private affairs of your mama and papa with strangers. After all, your mama and Uncle Harry might not wish it."

"Oh, it's all right," he returned earnestly. "Everybody knows!"

"I think," said Aurelia firmly, "that we should fly this

kite. Why don't you take it down into the garden and I will watch from up here."

"An excellent idea!" said a voice behind them.

Aurelia jumped and turned around. Harry stood just behind them, smiling. She wondered how much of the conversation he had overheard. Lest he should think she had been pumping the children for information, she said, "The children have just been telling me that their father is expected here tomorrow. I couldn't prevent them. I realise that you would not wish me to be a party to the affairs of your family."

"You could hardly ignore poor William's arrival," he said equably. "I expect him tomorrow and have assured him that, if he does not come, I will send to fetch him. I'll go myself if necessary! I have been engaged in engineering a reconciliation between my sister and her husband, and there is no reason why you should not know of it. It has been an exhausting process and I shall not rest easy until it is signed and sealed . . . and probably not then. I think I should have taken up a career in the Diplomatic! After dealing with Kate and William, I feel I am equipped to negotiate almost any treaty!"

"I am glad to hear it," Aurelia said, "because it must be better for the children."

"It is better for everyone concerned!" he said, then, obviously wishing to drop the subject, he offered her his arm and asked, "Will you not take a turn in the garden with me? I am very proud of Eastfield. I mean to show it to you in all its detail while you are here."

They descended the terrace steps and walked out into the sunshine of the garden. The twins were visible in the distance manoeuvering the kite, which was now flying very well, high above.

"Now there you have achieved something," Harry said. "I made them one, but it crashed immediately into a tree. Where did you learn the art?"

"Oh, I haven't made one for years," Aurelia said, "but my father used to make them for me. He was very good at that. They always flew. He explained the principle to me and I have not forgotten."

She fell silent as her mind ran back to a sunny, carefree childhood in a house where everyone lived for the day and no one had cared about tomorrow—*her* tomorrow. Harry, after a quick glance at her face, broke in on her thoughts. "Down this way," he said, pointing, "there is a fishpond. It was full of weed and mud, but I had it cleaned out and goldfish put in it. They seem to do pretty well."

They turned the path to the right and walked through a small clump of trees and found the fishpond at their feet.

"What a strange place for it!" cried Aurelia. "Why is it not nearer the house?"

"Because it is very old—older than the present house, I think. Not part of this garden at all. You see, over here there are the remains of some small building, I fancy a summerhouse. This stone seat is also very old. I think there must have been some kind of formal garden here when the first house was built in the Merry Monarch's day. In fact all the garden was laid out in a very formal manner, but my father had it altered to give a natural, English look."

"It must give you a feeling of great security," Aurelia said slowly, "to know that your family has been here for so many generations, and will be here for so many generations to come."

"Oh, I wouldn't predict the future," he said, stooping to pick up a small stone. "If I have no son, or daughter either, then I suppose I shall leave this place to one of Kate's boys. There is no one else. We are a family of women."

This had not occurred to Aurelia, but now she realised even more why the Fultons feared a marriage for Harry. Not only was there brother Harry, ready to pay bills, but there was Uncle Harry, so fond of the boys . . . fond enough to adopt one as his heir? Today the gift of a pony, tomorrow the legacy of Eastfield Park?

Harry tossed the stone he held into the pool and the gold and silver shapes gleamed in the water as they shot away in all directions. "Lazy creatures," he observed. "As soon as a shadow falls over their pool they come to the side because they hope they will be fed."

Much as Harry's relatives did, thought Aurelia. They all flocked to Harry's shadow to be fed.

Unexpectedly he asked, "Do you not feel secure, Aurelia? Jamaican planters can surely feel secure in their sugar cane wealth, and their houses are, I am told, very fine."

"My house in Kingston *is* very fine," Aurelia said. "And the house out at *Dos Amigos*."

"Where?"

"*Dos Amigos*. It's Spanish, and means 'two friends'. It's a very old name for the place. It's where the sugar estate is. We think the name is older than the estate and we do not know its origin."

"Then it is like my goldfish pool," he said, smiling.

But when the goldfish pool had been neglected and overgrown there had been a Harry to rescue it and lovingly restore it, thought Aurelia sadly, but no one was going to rescue *Dos Amigos*. She would have to surrender it and it would be sold. Strangers would come and live in the rooms where she had spent her childhood.

"Let us follow this path," Harry suggested. "It goes up the hill to that ornamental temple and you have a fine view from there. You can see all of the house and a large part of the grounds."

They walked on for some ten minutes, climbing a gentle gradient until they came to the summit of a low hill at the top of which had been built a pseudo Greek temple. When one came right up to it, it was found to be a cunningly disguised gazebo with a stone bench allowing the walker to rest and survey the panorama before him. Aurelia and Harry sat down and he pointed out the various local points of interest.

"That is the tower of St. Michael's church. It is worth the visit. When we go on Sunday you will see it. My father, grandfather and great-grandfather all have their memorials there, and in due course I dare say I shall have mine. I am seriously considering composing the verses myself, then I shall know what is said of me by future generations."

"How gloomy!" said Aurelia, smiling because he sounded so cheerful about it.

"A Gothic humour!" he said. "I have been spending my time, waiting for you all to get here, in reading Mrs. Radcliffe. And I have invented a ghost in the west wing of the house, solely for the benefit of my nephews." He pointed in another direction. "That is the home farm, and over there, where you see smoke, is the village. You can't see the cottages because my father planted those conifers precisely so that the village should be obscured. He was a man who liked his privacy."

Certainly, if any man wished privacy, he could not have it better than here in his own self-contained kingdom! Aurelia thought. Aloud she said sincerely, "It's truly a beautiful place, Harry. I know you said it was lovely, but I really didn't expect it to be like this. I don't know how you can ever bear to leave it and go up to London. It's so peaceful here, and quiet. Anybody would have to be happy here. It's the very best place to bring your sister and her husband because surely no one could be in disharmony in such a place as this!"

"And yet *you* could not live here, Aurelia?" he asked softly. "With me?"

Aurelia looked down at her hands. "It would be foolish of me to say no, Harry. Of course I could. But I may not. It just is not possible."

Her voice trembled and, try as she might, her words lacked resolution. Suddenly, she did not know how it happened, she was in his arms and he was kissing her. It seemed such a right and natural thing that they should do, and it answered such a yearning in Aurelia's own heart, that at first she could offer no resistance. But then she gave a sudden cry and pushed him back.

"No, Harry! Please, don't! You mustn't!"

He released her unwillingly, slipping his hands from her shoulders and seizing her wrists tightly in his fingers. "Aurelia, why do you refuse me? I am not blind or foolish. I wouldn't pester you with attentions which were unwelcome. I know that you are refusing me for some mysterious reason which you feel you cannot tell me. What is it?"

"Please, Harry," she whispered, "let us not talk of it any more."

"Very well," he said morosely, "then let us walk back. It seems that although I can hope to organise Kate and William's life together, I cannot hope for success in organising my own!"

He stood up and offered her his hand to rise. But Aurelia was staring down the hill, towards the house. "Harry, a carriage has just driven up to your door."

He turned quickly. "Where?" he asked, shading his eyes. "Good lord, it's William and a day early! His creditors must be dunning him. Come along, my dear, my presence as host is required!"

CHAPTER
TEN

THEY found Fulton in the library with his wife and Julia. Lady Belphege, it seemed, was resting and had not yet been told of his arrival. He was leaning against the chimneypiece and staring glumly at the packed bookshelves around him, as if he was already assessing the entertainment, or lack of it, which awaited him here. Catherine, in turquoise with lace trimmings, was again stretched beautifully on a sofa and had, Aurelia noted with some amusement, exchanged the red chaise-longue for a piece of furniture upholstered in blue silk, as being a more suitable foil for the ensemble she wore that day. Julia already looked exasperated and greeted Harry with visible relief.

"Well, well, Billy," said Lord Belphege cordially. "You are with us early!"

"I had nothing to keep me in Town," was the ungracious reply. The pouched eyes flickered from Harry to Aurelia and back to Harry again. There was something like amusement in the depths of them. "Good day to you, Miss Sinclair!" said Mr. Fulton meaningfully.

"Good day, sir," Aurelia returned awkwardly, wishing she had left Harry to greet his brother-in-law in the bosom of his family. "I trust your journey was agreeable."

"Damn' uncomfortable," he said. "But I dare say it don't matter, not to anyone here at least!"

There was an embarrassed silence broken by Lord

Belphege, who enquired, "You have not seen your children? They are outside somewhere, flying a kite which Miss Sinclair kindly showed them how to make."

"How nice of you, Miss Sinclair!" said Catherine coldly.

Now was definitely the moment for Aurelia to retire as gracefully as possible, and she did so hastily with a few muttered words.

Dinner that evening was a stilted, silent affair. Conversation was confined to small talk, and afterwards the four ladies retired to play whist in a drawing-room, leaving Harry and the increasingly gloomy Fulton to discuss the matter which had brought Fulton to Eastfield, in the library.

It could not be said that any one of the four card players was really concentrating on her hand. Julia constantly laid down the wrong card and Aurelia twice revoked. Catherine played competently, if with an absent-minded air, and Aurelia suspected that normally she was a very good player. Lady Belphege accused them all of inattention, but in a lacklustre tone which showed that her mind, too, was elsewhere. After a while the cards were put away by common consent and Catherine claimed a headache which took her up to bed, whilst Julia muttered something about letters to write and also retired. This left Lady Belphege and Aurelia seated either side of the fire, with the King Charles spaniel and an aged mastiff with bandy legs and almost no teeth slumbering on the carpet between them. Lady Belphege stirred the mastiff idly with her cane and he groaned in his sleep.

"That is truly a disgusting animal," she said, "but my son is unaccountably attached to it. You have probably noticed, Miss Sinclair, that this house is full of elderly dogs which should all of 'em have a stone tied around their necks and be dropped in the river! However, my son cannot be persuaded to part with any one of them. If you go out to the stables you will find an equal number of aged horses. I don't know why he must keep all these old creatures. Feeding them alone must cost him a considerable amount. Do you know, this mastiff can eat nothing but bread and milk, and it must be put up for him specially every day?"

"I think it very fine of Lord Belphege to look after animals which have served him well, when they are no longer of use to him!" said Aurelia stoutly.

"I dare say," returned her ladyship. "If he confined his charity to dumb beasts it would be something. But he must needs extend it to the wretched Fulton too! I cannot abide the man! I admit I did not disapprove the marriage, but then I thought Catherine had more sense than she has proved to have. If she concentrated less on charming all about her, and more on charming her own husband, I dare say things would not have come to such a sorry pass. You will not make the same mistake, I hope, Aurelia!"

"I trust not, ma'am," Aurelia said, a little awkwardly.

"Marriage," said Lady Belphege carefully, "can be a most difficult relationship. I would never wish to disguise the fact. Nevertheless, when based upon affection and mutual respect, it can provide the best basis for a contented and satisfying life that has ever been invented! It is always of greatest importance to choose a husband or a wife most particularly, my dear, and not be tempted into making a foolish match for all the wrong reasons!"

"No, ma'am."

"*Your* thoughts have not turned to marriage, my dear?" enquired the lady pleasantly.

Aurelia hesitated too long before she said, "No, ma'am. Not yet."

Lady Belphege gave her a very sharp look. "You should be thinking of it, my child. When a young girl is in the full flower of youth she should not waste the advantages which Nature has showered upon her."

"You flatter me too much, madam," Aurelia said. "If I have any looks, then I don't think they entitle me to imagine I can pick and choose."

"Why ever not?" asked Lady Belphege calmly. "If you were plain, my dear, you would not speak so disparagingly of being pretty! You have a very nice way with you, Aurelia. You are unaffected and intelligent and you have strength of character. As your poor late mother's girlhood friend, I hope you will allow me to speak freely?"

"You have been more than kind to me, madam," Aurelia said. "I hope you believe that I shall always be grateful for what you have done for me. It has been far more than I had any right to expect. Indeed, I had no right to expect anything or to ask anything of you. You would have had every justification for turning me from your door."

"Tush, child, what nonsense! I have been more than pleased to take an interest in you! But now we must look ahead, Aurelia. The season will be over when we return to London. Indeed, perhaps we shall stay here at Eastfield until next spring, when we may go up for next year's season."

"Oh, I couldn't do that!" cried Aurelia, so emphatically that the King Charles spaniel awoke and jumped up, yapping furiously. "I couldn't stay so long."

"You must stay somewhere, Aurelia. You cannot be roaming around London alone. We might write to your relatives in the West Country, of course. But I fear you would find an entire winter snowed up in an isolated house somewhere on the moors very tiresome, especially in company with a set of people for whom you might not care. However, for a young girl to return unmarried, season after season, is embarrassing and hardly the done thing. I—ah—have noticed, my dear, that my son shows a distinct interest in you. I have long wished to see him married and I would like you to know that I would consider you a most suitable bride for him. Perhaps the notion does not suit you."

"Indeed, madam, I would be very foolish if I said that the notion was disagreeable. I . . . I have a great respect for Lord Belphege and I am, I am very grateful for all the kindness he has shown me, including his hospitality to me here. But . . . but, as I have already explained to him in person, I really can't marry him! I'm sorry, Lady Belphege. I would certainly wish to oblige you," concluded Aurelia miserably.

"I would not wish you to marry just to oblige me," remarked Lady Belphege. "But I hope you will reconsider the matter." She hauled herself to her feet with difficulty. "Winter must be coming. I always feel the approach of cold weather. Good night, my dear!"

"Good night, madam," said Aurelia soberly. She sat down as the doors closed behind Harry's mother and wondered whether those last words really had been just a remark about the weather, or perhaps something more. A warning? A reminder that youth and beauty do not last? That even Harry's interest might grow cool or his attention be taken by another pretty face next year, in the next season? "It is hardly fair," said Aurelia to the spaniel, scratching his head, "for men go on being eligible until they are middle-aged, and a woman is accounted a failure if she doesn't secure a husband in one season! Not that I came looking for a husband. Really, it is too ironical. London must be full of girls trying to catch the eye of Harry and others like him, and here I am, with no wish to marry and nothing but a lot of debts to bring a husband anyway, and it seems I might have Harry just by smiling at him!"

She sighed. Life played cruel tricks. Harry wanted to

marry her. His mother wanted him to marry her. She herself would be the happiest person in the world if she could marry him. But she couldn't. And why? thought Aurelia, scowling into the fire. Because I have been so obsessed with my own selfish problems that I have thought of nothing but saving *Dos Amigos* and the house. I have given no thought to others or to what their feelings might be, and now I shall lose both Harry *and Dos Amigos*. It is not life that should be blamed—it is entirely my own fault. My own stupid, short-sighted, idiotic fault! And now I am the most wretched person alive and have no one to blame for it but myself!

She knew that if she did not rouse herself from these unhappy thoughts she would very soon give way to tears, and that would never do. She went to the card table and took the pack from its box and lay out the cards for Patience. But even that was doomed, for she could get none of the aces out and turned up red cards when she wanted black, and black in place of red, and it was all so frustrating that she pushed them all together and jammed them back in their box. "I shall get a book from the library and go up to bed!" she declared. But she could not do that either, for Harry and Fulton were in the library. Aurelia glanced at a nearby clock. It had grown quite late. Surely the two men would not be still arguing away? It would do no harm, she thought, to go to the library door and listen for voices. If all were quiet she would creep in and find herself a book.

Aurelia took a candle from the mantelshelf and made her way down the dark corridor to the door of the library. The house was very quiet now. It seemed that everyone must have gone to bed. There was not a sound from the library itself, and she opened the door just a crack. It was very dark in the room. If anyone were still there, the candles would be lit. Emboldened, Aurelia threw open the door and marched in with her candlestick held high.

A solitary figure sat slumped in a high winged chair before the dying fire. His long legs were stretched to the glowing coals and he held an empty brandy glass in his hands. He turned his head toward the door and the figure which stood there holding the candle. "Aurelia?" he said.

She walked slowly over to him and put her candle on the table beside him. "You are very tired," she said softly.

His face looked lined and older. He gave a crooked smile up at her. "A little tired. A little drunk too, perhaps. I have talked myself hoarse with, or rather at, Billy, and now I am seeking consolation in the brandy bottle!"

"Don't do that," Aurelia said quietly, "it does no good. My father did that."

"Did he? Well, he wasn't the first. Anyway, I'm not drinking myself to death, just blotting out the memory of William for a few moments. Will you sit down and keep me company for a while?"

"I'll keep you company, but I won't drink brandy with you," she said. "You must first put down the bottle—and then I will sit down."

He obliged by pushing the bottle and glass away from him on the table and Aurelia sat down in the nearest chair.

"I came for a book," she said. "They have all gone up to bed. I thought you had gone too."

"It was my sisters, wasn't it?" he said, leaning back in his chair.

"They have gone up to bed, too," Aurelia said hesitantly.

"Pah! I know that! I meant my sisters warned you off, didn't they?"

"Why should you think that?" she returned awkwardly.

"I've seen the way they look at you. Julia keeps an expression like a stone lion, and Catherine has obligingly sheathed her very long claws and is purring like the cat that has had the cream. It was not only because of them, I take it?"

"No, Harry, it wasn't only because of them."

"I see. I thought there must be some other thing which rendered me totally unattractive to you," he said moodily, staring into the fire.

Before Aurelia could stop herself she had slipped from her chair down on to the hearth rug and was kneeling in front of him, and had seized hold of his hand. "Don't, Harry, don't! It isn't anything to do with you! You mustn't find fault with yourself. It is me, me!"

"Aurelia!" he pleaded, grasping hold of her forearms and pulling her towards him, "I love you! If there is something else keeping us apart, then tell me. I don't care what it is. I love you and I want to marry you!"

"I'll tell you what it is stands between us, Harry," she said quietly. "It is the one thing we cannot overcome. It is money. You have money and I do not. If we marry, everyone will say you are the victim of a fortune huntress. Everywhere we went people would whisper and laugh. It would be a scandal—and although I've only been a little time in England, even I know what a scandal in society means!"

She pushed herself away from him and scrambled to her feet. "It isn't any good, Harry. It just can't be." She stumbled out of the room and ran upstairs.

The next day dawned bright and clear. Aurelia sat up in bed and wondered if, when she went downstairs, she would find the carriage standing before the door to take her back to London. Last night, in an unguarded moment, she had allowed just enough of the truth to emerge to make Harry want to know the rest. And when he knew it . . .

At that moment the peace of the morning was broken by a series of terrified screams and the pounding of running feet. Aurelia leapt from her bed and ran to the door and flung it open. She was just in time to see a dishevelled young female in maid's mobcap and apron race past brandishing a duster.

"Whatever's wrong?" cried Aurelia after the disappearing figure.

"Them little devils has set fire to the house!" floated back down the corridor.

Certainly there was a very strange smell coming from the floor above and, as Aurelia stood there, a stray wisp of smoke drifted past. "Good heavens, it's true!" she cried, and seizing a shawl, wrapped it around her as she ran towards the source of the smoke and smell, which proved to be the nursery. As Aurelia pulled open the door she was struck by a cloud of evil-smelling smoke which made her cough and stung her eyes, completely obscuring her vision.

"Richard! Robert!" she called huskily, groping forward in the gloom.

From somewhere in the fog a splutter was audible, followed by a childish treble saying, "It's all right, there isn't a fire. Only smoke."

Aurelia stumbled to the window and wrenched it open. Smoke swirled past her out into the fresh air and the atmosphere in the room cleared. Two small figures in nightshirts were now visible standing by the fireplace, from which still belched isolated clouds of dark grey smoke and curious smell.

"Children!" said Aurelia sternly. "What have you been burning?"

"You see," explained Robert, "it's a long time to wait

for November the fifth, but we thought we would practise making a guy."

"We used an old shirt and a pair of Nurse's stockings," contributed Richard.

"And then," said Robert with simple logic, "we put him on the fire to see if he would burn."

Aurelia grasped the poker, and lifting the smoulder-ing Mr. Fawkes, or what remained of him, from the top of the fire, carried him carefully to the window and dropped him out into the garden below.

At that moment Harry, Fulton and Julia all arrived together in various stages of *déshabillé*. Harry had ap-parently reached the stage of tying his cravat when sum-moned, as a half-finished knot '*à la Byron*' showed through the green brocade lapels of the dressing-gown he had hastily wrapped around himself. His brother-in-law looked as though he had just been roused from his slumber, as beneath a dressing-gown of startling oriental splendour, covered in peacocks amid brilliant foliage, protruded a pair of bare feet thrust into slippers. Julia was cocooned in a curiously shapeless garment which looked as though it had done service for the past ten years and wore on her head, incongruously, a morning cap in crisp frilled muslin. One side of her face was distinctly pinker than the other, and Aurelia guessed that Julia had been experimenting cautiously with rouge when disturbed.

"Well, at least we are not burning down!" observed Harry after a quick glance round the room.

"What, may I ask," demanded the papa of the twins, "have you been doing *now* to turn the place upside down at this unearthly hour?"

"It was only a practice Guy Fawkes, and I've put him out the window," Aurelia explained. "The maid ran away without stopping to find out what it was. She is obviously a very silly girl. I'm sure the boys did not realise how much smoke their guy would produce."

Fulton groaned and, wrapping himself more securely in the oriental dressing-gown, turned and stalked away, abandoning his children to the justice of their Uncle Harry.

"Little pests," said Uncle Harry. "I shall deal with you later. Clear this mess up at once, do you hear me?"

The assembled company dispersed and went back to dressing, except for Mr. Fulton who went back to bed. He failed to appear for household prayers in the chapel at nine, but did deign to put in a tardy appearance at breakfast which followed, where he drank a great deal of black coffee and spoke not a word. The others all discussed the children's latest exploit whilst making their individual breakfasts. Lady Belphege confined herself to tea, dry toast and observations that 'boys will be boys'. Julia tucked into coffee and hot rolls, followed by a piece of plum cake, none of which Aurelia could not help thinking, would help Julia's already well-rounded contours. Catherine sipped elegantly at hot chocolate and nibbled at a piece of pound cake, and no one could have guessed from her bland expression that her children were under discussion.

Harry appeared sombre as he ate his way silently through a platter of cold cuts, and Aurelia studied him covertly over her tea-cup. His only contribution to the conversation was to comment, in answer to Julia's complaints, that his nephews seemed aware of their sins and disposed to mind their manners for a day or two.

"We cannot hope for more than two days' peace, I suppose," he added, staring with scarcely concealed irritation at his brother-in-law, who had produced a small flask from his coat pocket and was liberally lacing his coffee with its contents. Harry certainly made no reference to that other conversation which had passed between him and Aurelia the previous evening. Indeed,

Aurelia began to wonder if, now that the effect of the brandy had worn off, he even remembered it. She hoped that he did not.

As a punishment for the alarms caused by their actions that morning, the twins were forbidden to ride their beloved pony or to fly the new kite for a whole week, and banished to the schoolroom to translate pages of Caesar's *Gallic Wars*. Everyone else, too, disappeared on various errands and Aurelia found herself alone. She was rather surprised, after wandering about the house aimlessly for a while, to walk into the library and find William Fulton there.

"Forgive me, I didn't mean to disturb you," she apologised, preparing to retreat.

"Come in, my dear Miss Sinclair!" was the affable reply. "I swear you are the one person in the whole house the sight of whom does not fill me with gloom and despair. My mother-in-law lectures me, Harry dictates to me, Julia moralises and Kate . . . well, Kate does nothing but lie about looking charming and smiling at me, and generally making me feel like a worm."

He seemed in such an unexpectedly good humour, despite his sad straits, that Aurelia smiled at him and returned, "Your children at least could never fill anyone with gloom. They are delightful!"

"Delightful, you say? Good heavens, they terrify me! It is Kate's doing. They are thoroughly spoiled and have no idea of discipline."

"They have needed their father, perhaps?" Aurelia could not help but suggest.

He pulled a wry face. "Much notice they take of anything I say! Much notice anyone here takes of anything I say! You cannot believe how they have badgered me on the subject of my marriage. Do you know, ma'am? They have made me give her up."

"Give up your wife?" cried Aurelia, shocked.

He looked astonished. "Wife? Lord, no! My mistress. Nancy."

"Oh, I see," said Aurelia, blushing. "I thought . . . well, anyway, I am sure you have done right, sir."

He shrugged and half turned away from her to lean one arm negligently on the marble mantelshelf. "Oh, I know I have done right," he said carelessly. "For, to tell the truth, I was damn' tired of Nancy and her whims and tantrums. At least Kate don't go throwing vases at a fellow's head. Nancy has a temper like a Fury. It has cost a pretty penny to be free of her, for she wouldn't settle for less than a small fortune, but Harry paid it, and now it is done and she is paid off and out of my life and good riddance."

Aurelia found his words unpleasant. Miss Nancy may have had many faults, but she and Fulton had been on the closest terms for some time, and his manner of speaking of her now—especially in regard to her having been 'paid off' like a member of a ship's crew—seemed, to say the least of it, churlish. She became aware that he was studying her carefully and in a most familiar manner.

"You'll pardon my asking, ma'am," he said, "but I should be obliged to you if you could tell me exactly how you do stand in regard to Harry. Gossip in Town led me to think that an engagement was about to be announced, now it seems it is not. Yet here you are, at Eastfield."

"I am not here at Lord Belphege's invitation, but at that of his mother," said Aurelia angrily. "Whatever you heard concerning an engagement you heard wrongly. You, sir, surely know what little account gossip can take of the truth and how easily it embroiders a trivial incident to make it seem something more than it is!"

"Yes, I know all that," he said. "But I'm not blind. There is something between you, I'd stake my last guinea on it. You and Harry are not . . ." he waved his hand vaguely in the air, "you're not, you know, on close terms, then?"

"Certainly not!" said Aurelia stiffly. "Nor are we likely to be."

"Then I'm dashed if I can see what Harry is playing at!" he said boldly. He took his arm from the shelf and turned to lean his back against it with his hands thrust into his breeches pockets and stare at her. She recognised his manner now as that in which he had once scrutinized her before the milliner's shop. His change of approach was as transparent as it was sordid. Whilst she was just a pretty girl, she was 'fair game'. Only when, for a short time, he had believed she might marry his brother-in-law and thus acquire influence over his own life, had he been at pains to be apologetic and servile, attempting to redeem his image in her eyes and toady to her for her favour. Now he knew she was neither Harry's betrothed nor his mistress. His false courtesies and pathetic pleas that she should not misunderstand him were cast aside as no longer necessary. "Then where do you plan to go from here, Miss Sinclair?" he asked.

"Sir?"

"Come," he said bluntly, "you understand me pretty well, I think."

Aurelia flushed. "I hardly see that what I do is any concern of yours, sir."

He grinned at her suddenly. "I could make it mine, Miss Aurelia! You see, we are kindred spirits, you and I! There is something rum about us both! You have too much brain in your pretty head to be just another young girl dancing a jig to Society's tune. No, no, my dear, there is much more to you than meets the eye. However, you are a minx with spirit and I like that. We could do famously together, you and I!"

"Mr. Fulton!" gasped Aurelia. "Are you proposing to *establish* me?"

He laughed. "Why ever not, my dear? You could do worse. Ask anyone. Ask Nancy. Ask m'wife!"

"I wonder you have the effrontery to mention your wife to me, sir, in such a context!" exploded Aurelia. "You have barely been reconciled with her and here you are, a few hours later, looking for . . . for a replacement for your discarded mistress. You must be out of your mind!"

"Pah!" he said, unabashed. "It don't matter to Kate. Don't mistake me, I think highly of my wife. She's a match for anyone, is Kate. But a man can't spend all his time kicking his heels by his own fireside."

"Some men," said Aurelia icily, "manage to do so!"

"Then they are dull fellows, ma'am, and not worth their salt!" was his reply. Without warning, he took a step towards her and gripped her arm none too gently. "Come, miss, don't play coy! I know your business right enough!"

He had badly mistaken his quarry. Aurelia wrenched her arm free, swung up her hand and dealt him a resounding slap on his pallid cheek, marking it with four red fingermarks.

For a moment he stood silent and then his careless manner dropped from him like a cloak. An ugly look entered his pouched eyes, and with an oath he stretched out his hand to seize her shoulder.

There was the barest noise behind them and a sudden swift movement as Harry's tall shape interposed itself between Aurelia and his brother-in-law. There was a flurry and a crack as Harry's fist shot out and made contact with Mr. Fulton's chin. The luckless William staggered back, but lost his footing on the polished parquet and crashed full length on the floor, shattering a spindle-legged table in his precipitous descent.

"Dear me!" said Lord Belphege silkily, standing over the sprawling figure. "I trust you have not hurt yourself, Billy?"

William spluttered and felt his jaw.

"Aurelia," said Harry, not taking his eyes from the body at his feet, "perhaps you would be so kind as to look out of the window for a moment?"

Aurelia, who did not mean to miss any of what was going on, remained where she was and was rewarded by seeing Harry stoop and seize Mr. Fulton by his coat-collar, haul him to his feet and frogmarch him down the length of the library, spluttering and protesting, and out of the door.

"Dash it, Harry! You don't have to half throttle a fellow!" came in aggrieved tones through the panelling.

Voices and footsteps faded. A minute or two later Harry returned, adjusting his cuffs, and remarked, "I do apologise, Aurelia. It is not the sort of thing I would like to happen to you at any time, and certainly not under my roof."

"Poor man," Aurelia said seriously, "I really don't think he can help himself."

"No more can he. He can no sooner set eyes on an attractive female than he must be meditating dishonourable designs with every hope of their success. William's hopes are only equalled by his optimism and conceit!" said Harry forthrightly. "But thank you for being so sensible about it, Aurelia, and not fainting away on the sofa or setting up a screech for help."

"Oh, he was angry for the moment, but there is little he could do to harm me here," said Aurelia. "I wasn't frightened."

He gave a short laugh and said, "Poor Billy! His advances do not now command even a decent alarm!"

He strolled to the window, ostensibly looking out. Now, thought Aurelia, he will ask me to explain what I said last night, about not having any money. But instead he said, "I have received some letters from Town this morning. Tony Helliwell, whom we met in the Park once, has written to tell me he is coming down. I expect him within the next day or two."

"I see," said Aurelia after a pause. Still he did not ask her to explain her words to him the previous evening. Had he really drunk enough brandy for the incident to be blurred in his mind? Or was it courtesy which prevented his asking questions? Perhaps it did not matter. When Helliwell came he might have more answers than Harry had questions. Why was Helliwell coming? Because of Julia, perhaps? Aurelia seized on this idea. Perhaps Helliwell's coming had nothing to do with her. Why should it? Yet she had every reason to fear that name.

CHAPTER
ELEVEN

JULIA sat in her room and read, for the fifth time, the letter in her hand.

" . . . We cannot continue as we are," it ran, "or at least, I cannot. I am determined to face both Lady Belphege and your brother. My being obliged to go down to Eastfield on another matter altogether gives me an opportunity which we cannot hope to see repeated. If you love me, my dearest Julia, you will agree that this is our only course of action."

Antony continued in the same strain for two more pages. Julia read them, sighed and folded up the letter. She did love Antony. She wanted, more than anything, to get away from her mother's autocratic rule. But the mere idea of facing Lady Belphege's wrath made her feel almost physically sick with apprehension. Mother detested Antony and would never change her mind. And as for Harry . . .

"Here am I," said Julia aloud to herself, "thirty-two and plump and plain. I am being offered the chance of a whole new life and I don't have the courage to take it."

Mr. Helliwell arrived at the end of the week. He would have been astonished if he had realised the full gamut of emotions with which he was awaited. Harry was pleased and interested. Lady Belphege was extremely cross. Julia viewed his arrival with a mixture of longing and trepidation. Catherine was hopeful of a skeleton about to be revealed in Aurelia's domestic cupboard, and Aurelia herself was filled with a dull and nameless dread. However, despite the reason which had ostensibly brought him, that other motive pressed more heavily on Antony's mind. At the earliest opportunity he sought out Julia alone and demanded an assurance of her support.

"Oh, Tony, Mother will never agree!" wailed Julia. "You just don't know her! When she has made up her mind on a thing, there is no moving her. If I thought we might have Harry's support it would be something. But how can I tell Harry I want to be married? At my age and in my situation? I have been over thirty years tied to Mama. How can I ever consider a home of my own, let alone a husband? Harry would say it was impractical, and I am dreadfully afraid that he would be right."

"What about me?" demanded Antony, looking a little annoyed. "It is all 'Mama will not' and 'Harry would not' and 'I cannot'. . . . what about me and what I should like and how I feel? For a whole year now, Julia, I have hung about Hyde Park in all weathers to meet you for a miserable five minutes. I have crept in and out of your mother's house like a . . like a servant who has been absent without leave. I have inveigled my way into your mother's parties. I have been pushed out of a window into a bed of rose bushes. I have been deceiving Harry, whom I have known for years, and whom I would not blame for calling me out!"

"Oh," Julia turned even paler, "he would not do that! Surely Harry would not fight you?"

"More likely to set the dogs on me!" said Mr. Helliwell gloomily. "Well, I have had enough of it, anyway. I mean to speak to him and to your mother. If you do not wish me to, then say so now. But remember this, I shall take it as a mark of dismissal! I shall assume you no longer care for me and that you wish our acquaintance to end."

"Oh, no, Tony, I don't!" cried poor Julia, wringing her hands. "But if Harry and Mama both refuse their consent and turn you out, then we should never meet again anyway. I couldn't bear it!"

Mr. Helliwell straightened his shoulders. "I am not so easily dismissed, my dear. I am prepared to argue with Harry and with Lady Belphege!"

"If you get the chance!" said Julia deflatingly. "Especially with Mother."

"In fact," Antony said thoughtfully, "I fancy Harry may give me more trouble than the old lady. Especially after he's heard what I have to tell him about Miss Sinclair."

"You have news!" Julia cried, darting forward. "What is it? Who is she? What is she up to?"

"Now, see here, Julia," he protested awkwardly, "You can't expect me to tell you before I tell Harry."

Julia took a step back and stared at him in astonishment. "Not tell me? But I asked you to find out."

"So did Harry. And he asked me first. Besides, it concerns Harry more than it does you, Julia. I know you're worried about him and all that, but it is Harry's affair, after all." A slightly mulish look had entered Mr. Helliwell's expression. "I'm sorry to disappoint you, my dear, but you surely realise I cannot give adverse information about Miss Sinclair to you before I speak to Harry or, come to that, before I speak to Miss Sinclair!"

Julia pounced. "Adverse information? Then she *is* false!"

"No, she ain't. I mean, in a way she is, but not altogether. See here, Julia, if I tell you any more I'll end up telling you everything. Now don't badger me about it, there's a good girl. I'll tell you later."

Julia saw that it was no good and reluctantly accepted the situation. "Then you will go to Harry now?" she demanded.

"No. I'll go to Miss Sinclair," was his reply. "It seems to me that is the right thing to do."

"She'll twist you round her little finger," Julia remarked bitterly. "She's able to do that to them all."

"Oh, I doubt it, my dear," Mr. Helliwell said knowledgeably. "I doubt she'll be pleased to see me, though."

Aurelia was walking alone in the garden; alone, that is, except for some very unsettling thoughts. It was all very well being prepared to face it out, no matter what happened. But here at Eastfield she was, as it were, marooned in the bosom of Harry's family. She could not sweep up her bonnet and shawl and stalk out. Even less could she creep away quite unnoticed by either family or servants. There was the matter of Sarah, and her boxes. There was the fact that she had no carriage of her own and was miles from London. Any departure required preparation and upheaval—and the co-operation of her hosts.

"If it must be done, then it can be done," muttered Aurelia sternly. "It's only a matter of discovering how!"

So absorbed was she in solving this daunting problem, that she failed to notice the approach of the gardener's boy and narrowly missed being run over by a barrow loaded with dead leaves.

"Beg pardon, miss!" said the boy.

Aurelia stared first at the russet and yellow pile of leaves which reminded her forcibly how late in the year it was getting, and then at the gardener's boy. He was a very large youth with spiky hair and a grimy smock and gaiters. His ears stuck out alarmingly from either side of his head and framed, like twin handles, a pair of eyes which were round and bright blue and at the same time contrived to be curiously blank. The gardener's boy was inclined to take life as it came. If the young lady wanted to stand in front of his wheelbarrow and stare at him, well then, let her. It did no harm. He only hoped she wasn't about to ask him some question which he couldn't answer.

"What is your name?" enquired Aurelia thoughtfully.

"Job Willis, miss!" said the gardener's boy, glad that the expected question was so straightforward.

"Job," said Aurelia, smiling at him encouragingly, "if local people, I mean in the village, want to go to town, how do they get there?"

Job released the handles of the wheelbarrow and reflected. "They walks, miss," he said at last.

"But it's very far!" objected Aurelia.

"They starts early," said Job.

"Is there no kind of conveyance?" An alarmed look entered the round blue eyes and Aurelia quickly amended her question to, "Isn't there a cart or a waggon to take them?"

"Oh, ah!" said Job, his expression clearing. "There's carrier's cart. Goes by on a Monday and a Friday. Or sometimes a waggon is going in from one of the farms, like."

"But the carrier goes past regularly on a Monday and Friday?"

Job said he did.

"Now then!" said Aurelia briskly. "Supposing anyone should want to get to London?"

"No one round here goes to Lunnon," said Job promptly. "'Cepting his lordship. Local folk never goes anywhere, only into Basingstoke, mebbe. Some of 'em don't even go there." He noticed that the young lady's face was registering some dissatisfaction, so he added obligingly, "There's mail coach. That changes horses up at the Fox and Hounds on the high road, other side o' the turnpike."

Aurelia seized on this. "And does the carrier call at the Fox and Hounds?"

"He would, miss, if he was asked."

Aurelia beamed at him. There, then, was her escape route from Eastfield! Should she need it, of course. Only one thing remained. "Do you think, Job," she asked him tentatively, "that you could carry a couple of boxes in your wheelbarrow?"

Job studied his wheelbarrow. "I dare say, miss, if it didn't have no leaves in it."

"Splendid!" said Aurelia. "If I should need you, Job, I shall send a message to you."

"Very well, miss," said Job philosophically. He did not wonder what the message might be. If she sent one, he'd find out quick enough.

They parted on terms of mutual satisfaction. Aurelia, her spirits considerably lightened, made her way to the goldfish pond and sat down on the old stone seat feeling almost cheerful.

"Good morning, Miss Sinclair!" said a rather diffident voice.

"Oh!" said Aurelia. "Oh, it's you, Mr. Helliwell."

"Yes, ma'am." He cleared his throat and added awkwardly, "I'm glad to find you alone, Miss Sinclair. I was hoping to—er—have a word with you."

"Sir?"

"I find myself in a very awkward situation, Miss Sinclair," he admitted, turning his hat in his hands. "I confess I would as soon not be in it." He made a stocky, solid figure in his bottle-green coat and nankeen breeches. He looked immovable, unyielding, dejected and obstinate. A man with his back to the wall, a man determined to do his duty or perish in the attempt.

Aurelia's heart sank like a stone, but she was determined not to show any sign of weakness before this man and managed to reply tolerably calmly, "You obviously have some matter weighing heavily on your mind, sir. It would oblige us both if you could unburden it as quickly as possible."

"Upon my soul!" he blurted out. "You have a cool manner for someone in a pretty tight situation, ma'am!"

"Am I in a tight situation, then?" demanded Miss Sinclair, knowing full well that she was.

"You know it at least as well as I do, I think" he said somewhat rudely. "You have been the subject of much correspondence lately, Miss Sinclair. I have written to my father. My father has written to me. He also sent a letter he had lately received from Jamaica, from an agent named Ribble. You know Mr. Ribble, I think?"

"We've met," said Aurelia noncommittally.

"Ribble apologises in his letter for not writing earlier, but it seems he has had the fever."

"I'm sorry to hear of it," said Aurelia. "I hope he's quite better?" Try as she might, she could not sound sincere.

"Presumably—since he was able to take up his pen and write to my father and tell him you had left for England. Ribble thought you might present yourself before my father."

"Ribble was wrong. That was never my intention!" Aurelia snapped. "Since Ribble acted on your father's instructions, there would have been little point in my seeking him out!"

There was a pause. "Between my father and Ribble I think I am now pretty well informed about you, Miss Sinclair," he said at last.

"So I imagine!" was the icy reply. "Your father is in a better position than most to satisfy your curiosity, since he has done so much to contribute to my present circumstances!"

"*My* father!" he said angrily. "My father has done nothing but carry out a bargain made by *your* father!

You might look at your own family if you want to find the cause of your present distress, ma'am! However, what I very much want to know now is, just what do you hope to obtain from Lady Belphege and her son?"

"Nothing!" blazed Aurelia, jumping to her feet. "I suppose you now intend to go to Lady Belphege and show her your father's letter and that of the wretched Ribble!"

"No. I intend to go to Harry and show him, since it was Harry who asked me to make the original enquiries."

Aurelia turned as white as a sheet and collapsed on to the seat again, clutching at the stone arm. "Harry did?" she whispered.

"Yes, and understandably. When a young woman arrives from out of the blue and asks his mother to vouch for her to all her friends and acquaintances, he is obviously bound to check on that young woman's credentials."

"I did not ask Lady Belphege to vouch for me!"

"Didn't you? You asked her to introduce you. It's the same thing."

Aurelia was silent.

"Your behaviour has been dashed odd altogether, Miss Sinclair!" he went on in a rush of words. "Bless me, half of London believes you a sugar heiress. Can you imagine what will happen when the truth is out?"

"Yes," said Aurelia coldly. She could imagine it without difficulty. Lady Belphege would disown her publicly and she would be branded as an adventuress, just as Gussie had warned her. She should have listened to Gussie. He understood the world in which he lived and had tried to warn her. She, obstinately, had refused to heed his words.

Helliwell was looking a little embarrassed. He had expected denials, outrage, perhaps even pleading.

Aurelia's calm was unnerving. "I shall inform Harry, then," he said weakly.

"Do so," said Aurelia tonelessly.

He half turned away, hesitated and turned back. "I . . . I'm sorry, Miss Sinclair. It's a miserable business. I wish it could be anyone but me."

"Oh, go and tell Harry!" said Aurelia wearily. "What's the good of apologising to me?" She realised she was being uncivil and added in a constrained voice, "Thank you, sir, for letting me know your intentions beforehand." She bit her lip. It was humiliating to have to ask him for anything, but she needed time. "Sir, I would like to ask you something."

"Miss Sinclair?"

"Could you . . . would you . . . wait till tomorrow before you tell Harry?"

"Why?" he asked bluntly, suspicion crossing his face.

"Because . . . because I have matters to set in order too, Mr. Helliwell."

He turned her request over in his mind and at last said unwillingly, "Very well, ma'am. I'll tell him tomorrow morning. But I trust you will not use the time between to brew up some mischief."

Aurelia flushed scarlet. "No, sir. You have my word—if you will take it, that is."

"All right, all right!" he said and after twisting his hat in his hands for a few moments more, abruptly bade her "Good day!" and walked quickly away.

"My dear Tony," Lord Belphege said affably, "anyone can see you're not the bearer of good news, but please don't look so tragic! What's it all about?"

It was the following morning, another sunny if cool day. Following breakfast, at which Aurelia had made only a brief appearance before retiring upstairs again, the family had dispersed about its daily pursuits, and Mr.

Helliwell had adjourned to the library with his host. In fact, poor Antony could have wished himself miles away, preferably out in the open, galloping over the downs with the hunt. In his mind's eye he could hear the baying of the hounds, smell the turf churned up by flying hoofs and thrill to the call of the huntsman's horn. He wrenched himself back to reality and the book-lined library. "I did as you asked me, Harry," he said stiffly. "I wrote to my father about Miss Sinclair."

"I see." Harry drummed his fingers thoughtfully on the table-top. "Perhaps I ought not to have asked that of you, Tony. I have rather changed my mind about prying into Miss Sinclair's credentials."

"But you ought to!" blurted the other, red with confusion. "Dash it, Harry, it's an odd business!"

Harry narrowed his eyes. "Go on, Tony. You had better tell me all."

"All? Well, it all starts with Captain Sinclair. Goodness only knows if he was a real captain, or only gave the rank to himself. Anyhow, Father remembers him quite well. He arrived in Jamaica with his wife and rather a mystery behind him. But, you know how it is. The West Indies are full of men who have left Britain under a cloud. Why else should a man go out to a climate full of yellow fever and malaria? Unless, of course, he's sent there as a matter of duty. People there don't—well, they don't ask too many questions about a man's past. It's how he behaves once he's out there that matters."

"And how did Captain Sinclair behave?" enquired Lord Belphege, settling back in his chair, prepared to listen to a long story.

"Very odd," said Mr. Helliwell with feeling. "Even for Jamaica. Very odd. He had money when he arrived. Some said it was his wife's. She doted on him. Some said his family had paid well to be rid of him."

"A remittance man?" queried his listener.

"Maybe," Helliwell shrugged. "Who knows? Sinclair could close up like a clam when it came to questions about himself. One thing soon became clear, however. He was a gambler and a lucky one. One way and another, after three or four years he was pretty well set up. Fine houses in Kingston. Carriage and pair. Frequenting the best society. His wife had drawings of Paris gowns smuggled in from Guadaloupe for her dressmaker to copy. He'd also come by a sugar estate in settlement of a gambling debt."

"*Dos Amigos*," Harry supplied.

Helliwell looked surprised. "Yes, how do you know?"

"No matter, go on."

Helliwell went on. "From that moment on, whatever he had gained by gambling he set about losing in the same manner. His luck really turned sour. That estate, *Dos Amigos*, was his undoing. He had no idea how to run it. In any case, it was run down, suffering from over-cropping and needing nursing along for a few years. You have to know the sugar business. Sinclair couldn't have grown a daisy in a pot! Besides, he had a lot of liberal notions about how to treat his negroes. His field hands only worked half as hard as those on other estates. It was a wonder he got his crop cut and crushed at all. What's more, he freed all his household slaves because he said he wished to be surrounded by free men, black or white, wherever possible."

"Which did not make him very popular with his white planter neighbours, I dare say," said Harry.

"You can safely wager it didn't!" Mr. Helliwell retorted strongly. "They were ready to run him off the island! They said he was an Abolitionist."

"I'm beginning to take to Captain Sinclair," remarked Lord Belphege.

"Are you?" said Mr. Helliwell gruffly. "Then listen to this! Not content with being the only man to lose money in sugar when everyone else was making a fortune, Sinclair had to meddle in other matters about which he knew almost nothing. He took a partner, a thorough-going rogue, fitted up a couple of merchantmen and traded around the islands and across to the Carolinas and back." Antony paused and bit his lip in some embarrassment. "Not all his cargoes were quite as they should have been."

"A smuggler?" demanded Harry with interest.

Mr. Helliwell wriggled. "We-ell, let's say for a price Captain Sinclair would turn a blind eye and carry your cargo, no questions asked. To be frank, he almost certainly did indulge in some out-and-out smuggling on his own account too. But he continued to lose money. It flowed through his fingers. He was in debt. His partner no doubt cheated him, but, as the business was scarcely legal, there was little Sinclair could do to obtain his fair share. What he did do was to borrow heavily on the strength of his properties and was given fifteen years to repay the loan. That was a legal agreement, all above board, cut and dried. Things went on for a few years, gradually going from bad to worse. The Sinclairs stopped living in style. They were no longer invited to the best houses. And then the crowning disaster . . ."

Harry leaned forward in his chair.

"As you know," said his visitor delicately, "there has been no success in outlawing slavery in the West Indies as yet. However, since 1807 it has been illegal to actually import slaves to the islands. But there are plenty who do not consider themselves bound by that, especially foreigners, and there are a few fortunes being made even now by smuggling slaves into Jamaica and the other islands. It's a dreadful business, but it is lucrative and unless you catch your smuggler red-handed, what can you do? There has been smuggling going on in the Caribbean since Drake's day. The islands are full of deserted coves and quiet landing places."

"I've heard of that," Harry agreed. "But surely Sinclair, with his abolitionist tendencies, didn't carry on such a business? I imagine him landing a few bales of tobacco from the Carolinas, but surely not slaves?"

"Sinclair did not. Unfortunately his partner did, though a complicated arrangement with Spanish traders. Poor Sinclair had reached the stage where, it seems, he was scarcely to be found sober, and certainly was no longer capable of keeping an eye on his partner. In 1810 a British naval ship intercepted what her captain took to be an ordinary smuggler off the coast of Cuba, making sail for Jamaica. When hailed, she tried to outrun them, but was eventually boarded. The hold was found crammed with human cargo, and Sinclair's partner himself was on board, very much in charge.

"Nothing could be proved against Sinclair, of course. Indeed, no one seriously thought the poor man even suspected what his partner was about. No one who knew him, that is. But think what his enemies could make of it, and did! He had enemies, too, by Jove! Plenty of 'em. 'So Captain Sinclair, who has treated us to his liberal views and preached emancipation at us, is nothing but a slave trader!' they crowed. 'A hypocrite of the first water!' Oh, they made the most of it. It broke poor Sinclair in every way. One can't help but feel sorry for the wretched fellow, though he brought ninety per cent of his troubles on himself. An odd mixture of a chap in lots of ways, Sinclair." Helliwell paused on this observation to take breath.

Lord Belphege was not a man to be misled by interesting red herrings. "No doubt,' he observed drily. "But what really brings you to me, I think, is not Sinclair's fascinating life, but the condition of his estate after his death."

"Precisely," said Mr. Helliwell. "He never repaid a

penny of his loan. After the scandal of 1810, he took to the bottle more than ever and would have drunk himself into the grave, had not yellow fever, of all things, put him there first. He left his misfortunes to his wife and daughter. His wife was in poor health and a broken woman. She died soon after."

"Leaving Aurelia alone with an encumbered estate and no doubt numerous other debts."

"I'm afraid so, Harry. She was frank enough in declaring her intentions to Ribble, our agent. There is little doubt that her object in coming to London and passing herself off as a rich sugar heiress, was simply to raise money. No doubt, sooner or later, she would have found a backer."

"And when, do you know, will the fifteen years be up?" enquired his lordship stiffly.

"December 31st, 1818. This year," returned Antony promptly.

"You speak of *your* agent," his lordship continued in a voice which had become very hard and cold. "Your father, forgive me if I leap to conclusions which are unfounded, your father seems very well informed as to Sinclair's debts and those of his daughter. May I ask who advanced Sinclair this notorious loan? Who will take all Aurelia owns if she cannot repay?"

Antony shuffled his feet and looked wretched. "Dash it, Harry. As to the last part of your question, in a way you could say, I will!"

CHAPTER
TWELVE

"But this is quite ridiculous, my dear Julia!" cried Catherine, barely troubling to hide her anger. "You should have *made* Helliwell tell you!"

"I'm sure I don't know how I'm to make a man tell me something if he doesn't want to," snapped Julia, nettled.

Catherine took a long look at her sister. "No," she said at last in a voice loaded with meaning, "*you* wouldn't."

Julia flushed. "I'm glad of it. I am not a hussy!"

"Pah!" returned Catherine bitterly. "There is your precious Antony in possession of information vital to us all, and you do nothing but congratulate yourself on your own virtue. Really, sister, you quite make me despair!"

They faced each other across Julia's bedroom. As soon as Harry had borne Antony away to the library, Catherine had run upstairs and trapped Julia in her room with a demand to know what Mr. Helliwell would have to say to their brother. To be told that Julia simply did not know had first filled her with incredulity, then fury, and now gloom.

"Why should it matter to you now, anyway?" demanded Julia, roused to real anger. "You are reconciled to William, are you not? William is to reform, we are told. Surely you do not still hope that Harry will keep you all?"

Catherine clenched her fists so tightly that the rings on

her fingers stood out sharply above white knuckles. Then she turned aside and stared with a glowering countenance at the window. She said nothing.

"You seem distressed, sister," observed Julia bitingly. "Where is that languid manner, that romantic charm we all know and love so well?"

"Oh, be quiet!" snapped Mrs. Fulton brusquely. "I am trying to think! How can I do so with you bleating like an ewe in the background? Now then, you are sure that Helliwell has information that will discredit Miss Sinclair?"

"I believe so. He indicated as much," Julia said stiffly.

"Then the question is," Catherine mused more to herself than to her companion, "how much does Harry love the girl?"

"Not at all!" cried Julia indignantly.

Catherine heaved a sigh. "Must you be so naïve, sister? Of course he loves her. Why else should she be here? But does he love her enough to overlook any scandal or deception?"

Julia looked unhappy. "I don't know." Her voice took on an obstinate note. "Harry is so sensible. Harry knows that if he marries he must think of the title. He must think of his heir. He would do nothing foolish!"

"Harry is a man, isn't he?" was her sister's reply to that. "Dear Julia, you fancy you know Harry, but you only know him as a brother. Miss Sinclair sees him as a lover! Good heavens, if our own Prince Regent could marry in secret to displease his father and risk the throne of Britain, then I'm sure a mere Viscount can be lured into a match with a planter's pretty daughter with a roving eye and a quick brain! Men have no sense at all when they fancy themselves in love. Only look at my poor husband, who has made a fool of himself time upon time again!"

"There is some difference between Harry and William

Fulton!" Julia returned savagely.

But Catherine was not listening. She had turned back moodily to the window. Suddenly her attitude stiffened and she hissed, "Sister! Come quickly! Look here!"

So urgent was her tone that Julia hurried to join her at the window. Silently, Catherine pointed down to the garden below, where a curious little procession was wending its way stealthily towards the main drive. It consisted of Aurelia, accompanied by Sarah Fraddon who was clasping a wicker basket and looking as though on her way to a funeral, and followed by a rustic figure trundling a wheelbarrow containing Aurelia's two boxes, with a hatbox wobbling precariously atop.

"Whatever is she about?" whispered Julia.

"She's leaving!" Catherine replied incredulously. "She's running away! I would never have believed it of her." Her voice rose exultantly.

"Leaving?" cried Julia. "Then we must send down and stop her immediately!"

Catherine whirled round and grasped her sister's arm. "No!" she snapped fiercely. "Let her go. By running away she declares herself guilty. It is far better than anything Helliwell can say!"

"But Harry!" argued Julia. "He'll be so angry if we let her go."

"By the time Harry learns of her flight, she'll be gone and good riddance! Who is to know either of us saw her? Unless you tell him, Julia, my dear!" Catherine's voice sharpened warningly.

Julia shook her arm free. "Oh, very well. But although I want her gone as much as you, I can't say I like the manner of it."

Catherine shrugged.

Harry stared thoughtfully at the purple and perspiring Helliwell for a long time, then he said slowly, "Captain

Sinclair borrowed this money from your father?"

"Yes, he did," said Antony in a defensive manner. "Swore to repay. Father was generous enough to give him fifteen years to do it, but he never saw a penny. I knew nothing of this, for I was a boy of nineteen when the affair was concluded, and I admit frankly that I have as little interest in business dealings now as I had then! I admit I should have known, but I didn't. It is my father who will take possession of Miss Sinclair's properties. However, he is elderly and infirm and, although I have no wish to hurry him into his grave, the fact remains that I am his only heir, and in a year or two . . ." his voice trailed away.

Lord Belphege suddenly assumed a brisk manner. "In that case, Tony, I fancy you and I may settle this business between ourselves."

"Settle it?" enquired Mr. Helliwell cautiously.

"Yes. It is high time you took a little practical interest in your affairs, and you can start with this one. Write to your father and tell him that Miss Sinclair has found a backer who will clear her debts, if he will supply the necessary details as soon as possible."

"But she hasn't!" protested Antony.

"Indeed she has. Myself."

"You, Harry! Have you gone mad?"

"I don't think so, Tony. I wish to pay off the money Aurelia owes your father. It's a simple business transaction."

"I would hardly call it simple! Look, Harry," Antony's face grew, if possible, still redder, "I know the girl has taken your fancy—in fact, I'm sure she's probably a very nice young woman, even if she's, well, a little unusual. But if you saddle yourself with her affairs now, you'll never be rid of her!"

"So I hope," observed his lordship pleasantly.

Helliwell was silent for a moment, then he said dubiously, "I see. I'll write, then, and request the details, although I'm totally opposed to your idea. I doubt I'm doing the right thing, but if it is your wish . . ."

"It is."

"You will think it over, Harry, won't you?" urged his friend. "If you change your mind, let me know at once."

"I do not make hasty decisions only to reverse them later," Harry told him. "On your part, Tony, I'd be obliged if you told no one else what you have told me."

Antony avoided his eye and muttered, "I have to tell one other."

"Who might that be?"

"Julia," Mr. Helliwell said firmly. "She also asked me to enquire into Miss Sinclair's origins."

Harry looked annoyed and said sharply, "If Julia had any doubts about the girl, then she might still have trusted me to do what was necessary. I do take my responsibilities as the head of this family seriously and would naturally enquire about any stranger, male or female, who sought out my mother to scrape an acquaintance!"

"It wasn't on that account," blurted Mr. Helliwell, rather disastrously. "It was because she fancied . . ." He recollected himself in the nick of time and fell silent. Seeing Lord Belphege's steely eye upon him, however, he realised a statement of some import was expected so he cleared his throat, straightened his shoulders and declared manfully, "Harry, this may not be the best moment to tell you, but Julia and I should like to marry!"

His host raised his eyebrows slightly and with only the barest hesitation returned, "Congratulations!"

"Oh, well, thank you, Harry," said Antony, startled by the calm acceptance of what he had thought would be a thunderbolt. "You, um, don't object?"

"On the contrary, I heartily approve. All that surreptitious hanging about in the Park was becoming a bore. Have you—or has Julia, for that matter—spoken to my mother about this?"

"Ah, no, Harry," said Mr. Helliwell, looking dejected. "We are sure she'll refuse to hear of it. She dislikes me and she wants to keep Julia at home at her every beck and call. I don't wish to speak impolitely of your mother, Harry, but she is being very selfish with regard to Julia!"

"My mother is elderly and has come to depend on Julia," Harry told him. "She won't admit it, but she's afraid of being left quite alone, as it were. However, Julia is over thir'—I mean, over twenty-one."

"Julia is two years younger than myself," Antony said stiffly. "A state of affairs I find excellent. A giddy young bride, always wanting to go to balls and card-parties and operas and entertainments, would hardly suit me. Nor should I suit a young girl. A bright young female married to a dull fellow like me would have nothing left to do but to elope with the footman!"

The notion that his sister appealed to her suitor so much simply because she was so dull, so struck Lord Belphege that he was speechless for some moments. Eventually he managed to murmur, "You are hard on yourself, Tony. Why, you are excellent company."

"Not amongst women!" said Mr. Helliwell firmly. "And never have been. Until I met Julia, I was resigned to being a bachelor. But as soon as I set eyes on Julia, I knew she was the very woman for me."

"I think," said his proposed brother-in-law, reaching for the bell-pull, "that Julia had better join us."

"You understand how it is, Harry," Julia said bitterly, some minutes later. "Mama simply will not let me go."

"I understand, Julia my dear, but if you want to marry Tony here, Mother cannot prevent you. I'm afraid you must take your courage in both hands and face her down."

"I can't, Harry! I never could. She reduces me to a quivering jelly with two or three words and a terrible look." She caught at his hand and said desperately, "If you spoke to her, Harry . . ."

"My dear girl, you cannot hide behind me! Either you love poor Tony and will fight for him, or you prefer to remain with Mother, unable to call your mind your own!"

"Come now, Harry, you are being hard on Julia," objected Antony. "How can she tackle your mother? She hasn't the weapons for the fight. It would mean misery and humiliation for her."

"In that case there is only one thing for it. A special licence. You will present Mama with a *fait accompli*."

"Marry secretly, without her consent, against her express wish?" whispered Julia, horrified by the notion. "I couldn't do that, Harry."

"Of course you can," he said briskly.

"Whatever would she say?" Julia asked him.

"A great deal, no doubt," said her brother with a smile, "but she'll get over it. Probably respect you for it. Now then, I'll be a witness, that will help to spike Mama's guns, and let's see, yes, Aurelia shall be another."

"Aurelia Sinclair, a witness to my marriage?" cried Julia. "Never!"

"Julia," he returned mildly enough, but with a touch of steel in his voice, "You must cease to wage this vendetta against Aurelia. I can speak of this before Tony, as he is to be one of the family and in any case, he knows what I am to say already. I intend to marry Aurelia, my dear, and I will not be prevented either by you or by Kate. I will not have either of you meddling in the matter. You must make your peace with Aurelia.

After all, I cannot have my sisters bickering with my wife. I think it is fair that you should support me in *my* marriage, if I am to support you in yours!" he concluded half-humorously.

Julia glanced at Helliwell.

"Oh yes," Lord Belphege continued, intercepting the glance, "Tony has told me a great deal, and shortly he will tell you. It makes no difference."

"She's accepted you?" Julia demanded.

"No, my dear. She has refused me."

Julia gaped. "Re—refused?" She rallied. "But, if she has refused you . . ."

He held up a hand "I mistimed my offer. Then, I believe, she felt she must refuse me. Now I very much hope I may persuade her to accept me. I intend to ask her today."

"But you can't!" Julia cried. "She's gone!"

Harry leapt out of his chair, his face reddening angrily, and Julia instinctively fled to the shelter of Mr. Helliwell's strong right arm. "What?" thundered his lordship. "How, gone? What have you and Kate contrived?"

"Nothing, Harry, I swear! She went off by herself about an hour ago. I saw her through the window. I know I should have stopped her, but Kate said—"

"I can imagine what Kate said!" he interrupted her brusquely. "How did she go? She has no carriage! Did she send down to the stables for a conveyance?"

"Well, no, Harry. Really, it's very strange. She—she had her boxes in a wheelbarrow."

"A wheelbarrow?" roared her brother. "What the devil do you mean? Aurelia couldn't push a wheelbarrow with boxes in it!"

"There was a boy pushing it. One of the gardeners, probably, or a stable boy. I don't know."

"He can't push it all the way to London," pointed out

Mr. Helliwell in a reasonable voice. "Damn it, Harry, don't you see? She's making for the mail coach."

Lord Belphege flung a wild glance at the nearest clock and then dashed unceremoniously out of the room.

Josiah Tully, landlord of the Fox and Hounds, had a cork leg. He was a small, wiry man and his boast was that he was as nimble on one and a half legs as most men on two, and in this he was probably correct. Where he was less correct was in telling how he came to lose the lower half of his left leg. "Give for his blessed Majesty, King George the Third, at the battle of Aboukir Bay!" he would say with pride.

"Go on, Jos, tell us about 'un!" would cry the regulars.

Mr. Tully would oblige his guests with a stirring tale which ended in the loss of his leg and Admiral Nelson crying: "Who is that brave fellow?" This part of the story was especially touching and female listeners were frequently moved to tears. In truth, Mr. Tully *had* lost his leg at sea, but in an accident on the gun deck during a drill—and it was not Lord Nelson but a very much more junior officer who had cried out: "Who is that idiot?" However, Mr. Tully was far too good a businessman to be hindered by trifling inaccuracies. He told his amended version of the Tale almost nightly, and before it ended his listeners were certain to have re-ordered several times. Quite often strangers who heard it bought Mr. Tully a drink too, as if unaware that he had the inn's entire stock of beer and spirits at his disposal.

"Now then," said Mr. Tully to himself as he sat outside the Fox and Hounds with his good leg propped up on a chair and his cork one resting in the dust. "What's all this, then?"

He was awaiting the arrival of the London mail, but what had arrived was the carrier's cart with the unlikely load of a very handsome young lady, a lady's maid and two large boxes. All of this was being decanted before the Fox and Hounds. Mindful that business is business, even if it comes in an unexpected form, Mr. Tully stood up and stumped to meet the new arrivals.

"Good morning, madam! Here, you, lad, come and take these boxes! Mind the ground, madam, it's very uneven just here." Mr. Tully gave the carrier a meaningful glance and added, "Good morning, Mr. Fritby!"

"Morning, Jos!" replied Mr. Fritby. Catching the meaningful glance, he shrugged and shook his head, indicating that he was as puzzled about his fare as Mr. Tully was.

The fare herself supplied part of the answer. "I want to catch the London coach," she said.

"Then you've come to the right place, madam, and no mistake about that!" Mr. Tully assured her heartily, as he clumped briskly ahead of her into the inn. "Always on time, the mail. You won't have long to wait. The change o' horses is being got ready at this very moment out back, and in my very kitchen there's a beautiful stew o' oxtail and onions ready for the passengers. Perhaps you'd like a plate o' that while you're waiting?"

"No, thank you," Aurelia said hastily. "But I'd like some tea, if you have any, and perhaps I can sit in your parlour?"

"Make yourself at home in the Sun, madam!" cried Mr. Tully, ushering her into a dim, north-facing room. "Tea will come directly!" There was some tea somewhere, he remembered. He didn't have much call for tea. By the time the passengers on the mail coach reached the Fox and Hounds they were generally ready to call for something rather stronger. He caught his guest glancing at his cork leg. "Give for his blessed Majesty, King George the Third, at the battle of Aboukir Bay!" said Mr. Tully automatically. He was pleased to see that the young lady looked properly impressed. So she should. It wasn't every day one had a chance to meet a survivor of a famous victory. It can be noted that Mr. Tully had told the amended version of the Tale of the Leg so often that he had almost come to believe it himself. He installed Aurelia in the parlour and stomped happily away, preparing the tale in his head for a new listener.

Aurelia looked dispiritedly at the parlour chairs. They all looked dusty, uncomfortable and long abandoned. Eventually she selected the window seat because it gave on to the front yard of the inn, and she would be able to see the mail coach when it arrived. She banged the seat cushion with the flat of her hand and a cloud of dust arose. Aurelia shrugged and sat down gingerly. A little dust hardly mattered when she had a journey by mail coach ahead of her. That would render all the travellers begrimed and exhausted. She untied the strings of her bonnet, took it off carefully and put it on the seat beside her. Now all she could do was wait and pray that Harry did not discover her flight too soon.

She glanced uneasily out of the unwashed window panes. Beyond the yard the high road was deserted. As she watched, the carrier came out, wiping his lips, and clambered up on to his cart. Aurelia watched him shake the reins and whistle to his mare before rattling slowly out of the yard.

The door swung open and clashed against the wall and Aurelia jumped. But it was only Mr. Tully with the tea things which he placed before her with a flourish. "I trust everything will be to your liking, madam!"

"Thank you," said Aurelia.

"Stew is hot," said Mr. Tully by way of a hint as he withdrew.

Sarah put her head round the door. "Miss Aury! I'm just out here in the corridor, sitting on they boxes!"

"I don't think that's necessary, Sarah," objected Aurelia mildly.

"Well, I do!" Sarah said ominously. "Who knows what kind of folk they got round yere?"

Left alone again, Aurelia slowly poured herself a dish of weak tea and sipped it thoughtfully. She was wondering how long it would take to procure a passage to Jamaica. She resolved to enquire, when the coach reached Basingstoke, whether it was possible to travel from that town directly to Bristol. If it was, she would abandon the London mail and turn her travels westward. This would have the added advantage of confusing pursuers—if pursuit there should be.

At the thought of Harry, she put down the cup and looked uneasily out of the window again. Perhaps she was only flattering herself by imagining he would follow her. It was more probable, she reflected dismally, that he would simply shrug his shoulders and dismiss her from his mind as being too unreliable a person to bother about any more.

Outside the door, some altercation could be heard between Sarah and Mr. Tully. The landlord wished to move the boxes outside in readiness for the coach. Sarah refused adamantly to budge from her secure perch on them. There was little doubt who would win this contest of wills, but, distracted by the arguing voices, Aurelia allowed her attention to wander from the window. Suddenly, to her horror, the thud of hoofbeats heralding a single rider fell on her ear and to her complete dismay, the unmistakable figure of Lord Belphege astride a lathered horse galloped into the yard at breakneck speed. As his mount slithered and snorted to a halt, he leapt from the saddle to the ground, flung the reins at an astonished ostler and sprinted towards the inn door, shouting: "Tully! Damn you, where are you, man?"

Aurelia leapt up in alarm, spilling her tea on the table

top, but it was too late to escape. There was a stamp of feet outside, a shriek from Sarah, the door burst open and the tall, solid form of the Viscount Belphege filled the doorway.

Strangely, Aurelia's immediate thought was how much he looked now as he had done when she had first seen him; that was to say, angry. Only now the anger was redoubled. Glowering at her from beneath his thick black brows, he kicked the door shut with the heel of his riding boot and roared: "Devil take it, woman! What do you mean by sneaking out of my house with your baggage in a wheelbarrow?"

Aurelia opened her mouth, but, try as she might, she could not make a single sound come out of it. Her throat seemed struck by paralysis.

"Coming here by carrier's cart!" Harry thundered. "Do you realise that before long, half of Hampshire will ring to the legend of how I throw out my lady guests, leaving them to fend for themselves on the *mail coach*? Have you thought that at every stop the wretched carrier makes, he will relay the story of your flight—wheelbarrow and all—and I will be cast in the rôle of some kind of blackguardly villain?"

Aurelia blanched and found her tongue at last. "Oh, Harry," she stammered, "I . . . I never thought of it like that. I am so sorry."

"Moreover, madam," he continued, coming a step nearer, "do you propose to travel *alone* on a public coach?"

Aurelia shrank back against the wall. "Yes, Harry," she said weakly.

There was a silence during which Harry seemed to be fighting to regain his self-control. At last he said more quietly, but still very sternly, "You have behaved very badly, Aurelia."

"Oh, Harry, I have," Aurelia cried, "and you don't

know how badly! There's so much I haven't told you. I'm over my ears in debt. All my property is heavily encumbered and I'm about to lose the lot—to the Helliwells!"

"So I have recently learned!" he said heavily. "My dearest girl, I realised from the start that in fact you had precious little fortune, but I came to the conclusion that you only disguised that because you were afraid you would not be admitted into good society without a fortune behind you. You can imagine that I find it disagreeable, to say the least, to be informed that you have been flitting about London trying to persuade people to part with money for the sake of your pretty eyes!"

The pretty eyes flashed dangerously at him. "That's not what I have been doing! I asked only one person, and that was Captain Foote, and I explained about the debt."

"And he said?"

"He said he had no money and anyway, I shouldn't do it, I would get myself locked up," said Aurelia, less confidently. "But, Harry, it was a genuine business proposition! The properties are really an excellent investment. All the houses in Kingston are very good, if in need of a little paint and plaster. You may ask anyone. They will all tell you the same. Mr. Helliwell the senior would not have taken them as surety against the loan if they hadn't been worth it! It's the same with the estate at *Dos Amigos*, it only needs good management and some new machinery for rolling and crushing the cane. It could easily be made to repay the loan over and over again."

"Then why didn't it?" he demanded bluntly.

"Because poor Papa lost heart, especially after Da Costa behaved so badly by him."

"Da Costa?"

"His partner. Oh, a horrid man, Harry, with black

moustachios, just like a pirate! He cheated Papa all the time and then he did a dreadful thing—perhaps Helliwell told you of it. My papa was not a bad man, Harry, he was a good, kind man. But he was weak, and a gambler, and always believed in 'luck'. He always thought that, if only he had a little luck, everything would come right overnight!"

Her voice trailed away. "But you are quite right to be angry with me, Harry. It *was* wrong of me to mislead people, no matter what my motives were," she added very quietly.

He threw his hat across the room to land on the window seat beside Aurelia's bonnet. "Damn it, Aurelia," he said wearily, "of course I'm angry! But not about the money, about your running off!"

Aurelia bit her lip like a guilty schoolgirl and muttered, "I'm sorry, Harry, truly. But it did seem the only thing to do."

"For pity's sake, girl, why did you not at least ask for a conveyance back to Town, if you felt you must go? You really did not have to depart by wheelbarrow!"

There was a pause. Aurelia gave a stifled snort and Lord Belphege put his hand to his head. "Heaven help us all," he groaned. "Aurelia, that wheelbarrow will pass into local history! But only you would think of it!"

"You will not be angry with Job Willis, I hope?" Aurelia asked anxiously. "He meant no harm, only to oblige me."

"I don't even know who he is!" was the retort.

"He pushed the wheelbarrow," Aurelia informed him. "He works for you, in the gardens."

"He sounds a perfect idiot," said Lord Belphege.

"Well, he did seem not awfully bright," agreed Aurelia. "That's why I asked him to do it. I mean, if he'd been clever he'd have refused, or told you."

Conflicting emotions fought for control of Lord Belphege's features. Then he sat down suddenly at the table and put his face in his hands. His shoulders began to shake.

"Harry?" whispered Aurelia, alarmed. "Are you all right?"

He raised his head, his face convulsed with laughter. Then he composed his features and looked her directly in the eye. "Aurelia," he said with awful emphasis, "my honour is in your hands."

Aurelia looked startled. "Your honour? How can it be?"

"For the reasons I have put to you. What kind of a figure do you think I will cut after this?"

"I've said I'm sorry, Harry. I'll tell everyone it was my idea and my fault. What else can I do?"

"We shall have to be married," he said briskly. "There is nothing for it. Nothing else will stop the rumours."

"Oh, no, Harry!" said Aurelia quickly. "That's silly. Especially as . . ."

"Even now," continued his lordship, interrupting her, "the good mine host will have decided that everyone has heard enough of that ridiculous story about his leg and how he lost it in some battle . . ."

"Aboukir Bay," supplied Aurelia.

" . . . and he will be busy preparing the Tale of how Lord Belphege's intended Bride attempted Flight!"

"I wasn't your intended bride," said Aurelia.

"But you are now," he said artfully. "Now, don't begin to prattle about your debts. As I told you before, I have long been interested in acquiring property in a warm climate."

"No, Harry, please!" begged Aurelia. "Not you! I don't want money from you!"

"I cannot have my wife in debt," he said mildly. "And

certainly not in debt to the family of my sister's proposed husband!"

"Is she going to marry him?" asked Aurelia, diverted. "I did wonder."

"Are you going to marry me, Aurelia? That is more to the point!" He stood up and came round the table to stand before her. "Come, Aurelia," he said seriously, "you know I love you. I know I should never be able to love anyone else. We have but one life on this earth, as I believe, and are we two to spend it apart because of some sordid question of money? Must we sit on either side of the Atlantic Ocean, eating our hearts out, because we have not the courage to follow the promptings of those hearts?"

"No, Harry," Aurelia said quietly, "I do love you. But because I love you very much, I would never have people say I had trapped you into a marriage and make you out to be some sort of gullible simpleton who fell into the hands of an adventuress!"

"Given the choice of being a gullible simpleton or a dreadful scoundrel who drives out defenceless women from beneath his roof with their worldly possessions in a wheelbarrow, I willingly choose to be a happy fool." he said with a smile, slipping his arms around her waist. "So you will be my wife, dearest Aurelia, won't you?"

"Yes, Harry," said Aurelia, leaning her head on his chest. "Yes, please."

Masquerade
Historical Romances

Intrigue excitement romance

Don't miss
August's
other enthralling Historical Romance title

BUCCANEER'S LADY
by Robyn Stuart

Proud, but loving and impetuous, Corinna Barrett
sails from England to the West Indies in search of her
missing father, Lord Barrett. But ill luck makes her
fall into the hands of the pirate Ahab Quinn — to be
bought by Captain Brandon Hawke, a buccaneer who
hates and despises both Corinna and the corrupt
Restoration England she represents. Yet Corinna
finds a different sort of freedom in captivity, and it is
only when she is close to finding her father that she
realises the bitter choice she must make — to sacrifice
her self-respect, or lose the man she loves.

You can obtain this title today from your local paperback
retailer